...tham Forest...

...e loan may be
...r customer.

'I absolutely ADORED it! A really

brilliant play on all the Christmas tr...

It just has to be made into a movie!'

Emma Carroll

'Very sparkly storytelling and a lovely portrayal

of friendship'

Hilary McKay

'Joyful and hilarious. I loved every moment of it'

Stephanie Burgis

'*Tinsel* is Christmas spirit wrapped in a fun,

feminist parcel'

Lesley Parr

'A sparkling, glittering festive delight, *Tinsel* is funny,

warm-hearted and thrilling too – it made my toes

tingle and my heart glow with Christmas magic'

Sophie Kirtley

WALTHAM FOREST LIBRARIES

904 000 00708838

Books by Sibéal Pounder

Tinsel: The Girls Who Invented Christmas

Bad Mermaids
Bad Mermaids: On the Rocks
Bad Mermaids: On Thin Ice
Bad Mermaids Meet the Sushi Sisters
Bad Mermaids Meet the Witches (for World Book Day)

Witch Wars
Witch Switch
Witch Watch
Witch Glitch
Witch Snitch
Witch Tricks

Beyond Platform 13 (with Eva Ibbotson)

Tinsel

The Girls Who Invented Christmas

SIBÉAL POUNDER

BLOOMSBURY
CHILDREN'S BOOKS
LONDON   OXFORD   NEW YORK   NEW DELHI   SYDNEY

BLOOMSBURY CHILDREN'S BOOKS
Bloomsbury Publishing Plc
50 Bedford Square, London WC1B 3DP, UK
29 Earlsfort Terrace, Dublin 2, Ireland

BLOOMSBURY, BLOOMSBURY CHILDREN'S BOOKS and the Diana logo are
trademarks of Bloomsbury Publishing Plc

First published in Great Britain in 2020 by Bloomsbury Publishing Plc
This edition published in Great Britain in 2021 by Bloomsbury Publishing Plc

Text copyright © Sibéal Pounder, 2020
Illustrations copyright © Sarah Warburton, 2020

Sibéal Pounder has asserted her right under the Copyright, Designs and Patents Act,
1988, to be identified as Author of this work

All rights reserved. No part of this publication may be reproduced or transmitted in
any form or by any means, electronic or mechanical, including photocopying,
recording, or any information storage or retrieval system, without prior permission in
writing from the publishers

A catalogue record for this book is available from the British Library

ISBN: HB: 978-1-5266-1927-3; PB: 978-1-5266-1926-6; eBook: 978-1-5266-1925-9

2 4 6 8 10 9 7 5 3 1

Typeset by RefineCatch Limited, Bungay, Suffolk

Printed and b ... on CR0 4YY

WALTHAM FOREST
LIBRARIES

904 000 00708838

Askews & Holts	05-Nov-2021
JF STO	

To find ou ... sbury.com

A Note on Elves

Every year on Christmas Day in a snowy land far, far away, elves build snowmen and then burrow inside them.

Anyone who has studied elves (and no one has) will know that this is the most important date in the elf calendar, because it is the day that they get their elf magic for the year.

Anyone who has studied elf magic (and no one has) will know that unlike other kinds of magic, elf magic is not *made*. They do not brew it in cauldrons, like witches, or summon it from the skies, like sorcerers. Instead, elves are completely reliant on an ancient Christmas ritual known as Snowcus Pocus.

This ridiculous, cold and lengthy process – resulting in a limited quantity of magic – led elves to believe that their magic was the worst in the world. But they are sticklers for tradition and routine, and so every Christmas without fail they climb into their snowmen and wait for the important first snowfall of the day.

When the snow falls, the snowmen begin to glow, growing brighter and brighter. The technicolor icicles strung up around town flash as if the whole place has been dipped in a disco, and then the elves emerge, full of magic to last a whole year.

But elves are timid creatures and magic can be unwieldy. It scares them, so they almost never use it. Anyone who has studied the elf world (and no one has) will know that hidden in the North Pole is enough magic to make the wildest wishes come true.

Prologue

What do we know about 'Mrs' Claus? The truth is: *almost nothing*. She lives in the background of Christmas stories all around the world, and that is where we have kept her for hundreds of years. But what if, a long time ago, we got the story wrong? What if the truth disappeared out of sight, and she along with it?

It is a story she wanted people to know – a story of resilience and little acts of kindness. A story of *real* tinsel and how two formidable girls changed Christmas forever.

This is her story.

This is the story of Blanche Claus.

Chapter 1

The Bauble

Once upon a time – over one hundred years ago – there lived a girl with ice-white hair who truly hated Christmas.

The girl's name was Blanche Claus, and on this Christmas – the Christmas when we find her – everything seemed entirely ordinary at first. She was alone in London, huddled under the bridge she called home. Across the river, horse-drawn carriages danced along frozen streets, practically flying people to their destinations. She stared at the scene longingly. Everyone had somewhere to be on Christmas Day. Everyone except her.

Blanche, somewhat uniquely, spent her Christmases counting down the seconds until the day was over. Preferably as loudly as possible.

'Eighty-six thousand, three hundred and twenty-four! Eighty-six thousand, three hundred and twenty-three!'

Her parents had died before her memories began, and Blanche's life had been little more than a blizzard-blur of the city's orphanages, each one more ghastly than the last. But by the time she was four she was determined never to spend another night in an orphanage again. No matter where she was taken, she rarely stayed longer than an hour. Despite the bolted doors and barred windows, she always escaped.

How she escaped remained a mystery to everyone.

'Eighty-five thousand, one hundred and four! Eighty-five thousand, one hundred and three!'

She knew she wasn't one of the lucky ones – she was alone, and Christmas more than any other day of the year reminded her of that.

'EIGHTY-FOUR THOUSAND, EIGHT HUNDRED AND TWO! EIGHTY-FOUR THOUSAND, EIGHT HUNDRED AND ONE!'

Normally, the Christmas countdown would go on until the day was done or Blanche had fallen asleep, but this year was different. Something distracted her.

A cloaked old woman was hobbling in her direction.

Blanche halted her counting and waited for the woman to pass by, but she grew closer and closer until there was barely space for a snowflake between them.

A red bauble dangled from her finger.

'Hello?' Blanche whispered, her voice cracking like nervous ice.

The old woman pulled back her hood, revealing white hair just like Blanche's. Her eyes were cloudy, frosted over like the river. She leaned in closer.

'This is for you,' she rasped. And she held out the bauble for Blanche to take.

'For me?' Blanche asked, presuming a mistake had been made.

'For you,' the old woman insisted. 'For Christmas.'

'Thank you,' Blanche said quietly. 'I've never been given a Christmas present before. But … I should be honest – it'll be wasted on me. I don't have a tree to hang it on. You should keep it.'

'You don't need a tree for this bauble.'

'Then what will I do with it?' Blanche asked.

'Only you know that,' the old woman said mysteriously. 'Never underestimate the gifts you are given. What you see inside might surprise you.'

Blanche raised an eyebrow sceptically, but the old woman held the bauble closer. Carefully, Blanche lifted it by its gold thread and cupped it in her hands. She'd thought it must be a trick, but the bauble was impossibly cold. Colder than ice.

'Merry Christmas,' the old woman whispered with a smile, just as the red surface of the bauble began to swirl.

Blanche looked closer, peering past the shimmering streaks of festive colour to what lay beyond. She could see a snowy landscape decorated with tiny houses and technicolor icicles! And right in the middle was ... a giant dancing Christmas tree?

She blinked, convinced she was imagining it, but when she looked again it was still there. Its decorations clashed against each other as it twirled madly, making some of them fizz and shatter like fireworks.

'I-I-I can see—' she began, too excited to get the words out. 'It's—' She looked up at the old woman for answers.

But the old woman was gone.

Chapter 2

A Horse

The bauble was just the beginning.

After that, Blanche felt something change in her – a flurry of snow in her belly so strong she thought it might raise her up into the sky. Suddenly, it didn't seem right to spend the rest of Christmas Day under the bridge, counting down the seconds until it was over. The world inside the bauble had made her see that adventures were out there. The old woman had made her realise – if only for a second – that she wasn't truly alone. And the magic of holding on to one small thing that felt like it might just change everything was enough to make her stand up and start walking.

That day – that moment – changed Christmas for everyone.

With a new sense of hope, Blanche made her way across the bridge and into town. She walked past houses dressed for Christmas, with windows framing roaring fires and fat turkeys on tables. She had no destination in mind – she just walked. The empty streets were covered in fresh snow and she sighed happily. London felt like it was all hers. She had just started to dance, twirling through the silence and catching snowflakes on her tongue, when the most unexpected sight made her stop.

There was a horse standing alone in the middle of the road.

The poor thing looked abandoned, with her neck bent low and her ribs on show. She was shivering, so Blanche approached slowly, making a clicking noise, which she hoped the horse would interpret as friendly.

'It's all right,' she whispered, getting close enough to pat her neck. The horse flinched.

'Don't be scared,' Blanche said. She spotted a pile of empty sacks stacked on some barrels and began layering them on the horse's back for warmth. In one she found some old Christmas puddings and laid them out on the snowy ground for the horse to munch on.

'What's your name?' Blanche whispered, as if the horse might be able to answer. 'I can't just call you Horse.'

She waited a moment, then looked down at the writing on the sacks.

RUDY'S CHRISTMAS PUDDINGS.

'Rudy ...' Blanche tried out loud.

The horse neighed enthusiastically.

'Rudy!' Blanche cheered, nestling her face into the horse's wispy mane. 'Well, now that I know your name, I should probably return you to your owner.'

She began to look around, but Rudy whinnied loudly and shook her head from side to side.

Blanche stared. It was as if Rudy had understood every word.

'You don't have an owner?'

Rudy whinnied again and an idea began to form in Blanche's head.

'Well, if you don't have an owner, then ... would you like to come with me? I'll take care of you, always. I'll never leave you.'

Rudy nuzzled into Blanche and nibbled at the bauble sticking out of her pocket. Blanche took it as a sign.

'It's settled,' she said.

With an ear-splitting whinny, Rudy reared up, making Blanche leap back in fright! The horse began madly throwing her head up in the air as if trying to tell her something.

'What is it?' Blanche cried. 'What's wrong?'

Rudy spluttered impatiently and then tossed her head in the air again.

'Up?' Blanche said. She looked up to the sky.

Rudy stretched around and tapped her nose to her body.

'Oh, you want me to ride you? Is that it?' Blanche asked. 'I'm sorry, I can't. I don't know how to ride a horse.'

Rudy scraped her hoof on the ground and spluttered again.

'Don't be like that, it's not my fault,' Blanche said. 'I've never had the chance—'

Rudy interrupted her with another impatient splutter, then bit at Blanche's jacket, pulling her closer.

 11

'OK, fine!' Blanche said. With an awkward leap, she half jumped, half heaved herself on to Rudy's back and fell forward, grabbing a tuft of the horse's mane.

She lay belly down for a second, scared to move. 'Now what?' she asked. 'Should I try sitting—?'

Rudy shot off through the London streets faster than Blanche had ever seen a horse move. She held on for dear life, wincing as they dodged lamp posts and crying out as they skidded around corners.

'RUDY!' she shouted. 'HALT! SLOW! STOP! FREEZE! WHAT IS HORSE FOR STOP?!'

Rudy neighed and Blanche was sure it sounded like a chuckle. She clung on, dangling by nothing but frozen fingers on a threadbare mane.

The whole world leaped around her in rocky jolts that made her feel sick. It was obvious Rudy had no intention of stopping, so Blanche took a deep breath and raised herself to a sitting position.

As soon as she did, the horse's heaving movements evened out and Blanche felt as if she and Rudy clicked into place.

'AM I HORSE RIDING? IS THIS IT?' Blanche cried. Rudy glanced back and winked.

They thundered on, and it wasn't long before Blanche began to enjoy herself. For the first time in years she was grinning from ear to ear.

'TALLY-HO!' she roared, just as something leaped into view, making Rudy rear up in fright. Before Blanche could do anything, the horse disappeared from under her and she tumbled backwards into the snow.

When she opened her eyes, slush blurred her vision. A watery outline of a figure swayed in front of her.

'LEAPING CHRISTMAS TREES! ARE YOU ALL RIGHT?!'

Chapter 3

The Corner Where Christmas Trees Are Sold

Two hands tucked under Blanche's armpits and hauled her upright. She hastily rubbed the snow out of her eyes, and the second surprising sight of the day came into focus.

It was a girl, around the same age as her, wearing the most unusual outfit Blanche had ever seen. The edge of her tattered skirt was trimmed with crumpled wrapping paper, and baubles hung from her ears. Her filthy jacket had a broken angel decoration stitched on to it like a brooch and her long dark hair was pulled into a plait wrapped with wilted mistletoe. It looked as though she'd been all over London picking up stray bits of Christmas.

'Your outfit,' Blanche said, 'is SPECTACULAR.'

The girl smiled and did a little bow. 'Why, thank you very much.'

'Where did you find all those things?' Blanche asked.

'Oh, on the street, mostly,' the girl said. 'Most of them were lost. That's why I wear them – so their owners can easily find them again!' She patted Rudy. 'I'm truly sorry for startling your horse. I LEAPED up and I don't think the horse expected it … I just got so excited when you came true.'

'When I what?' Blanche asked.

'Came true! You're my wish!' the girl said, hugging Blanche tightly. 'I didn't expect you to be delivered so quickly. Only seconds ago, I said to the snowy sky, "PLEASE CAN YOU SEND ME SOMEONE TO HAVE A MINCE-PIE PICNIC WITH?" And BOOM-SPLAT here you are! I think you're wonderful already and I've only known you for two seconds. I'm Rinki, and I would love you to join me for a mince-pie picnic.'

'Me?' Blanche managed, completely overwhelmed. She tucked her hand in her pocket to touch the ice-cold bauble again. 'I would love it,' she said quietly. 'I've never had anyone to spend Christmas with, and I've never been to a … um … what did you call it?'

'A mince-pie picnic!' Rinki cheered. 'It's only the best Christmas tradition *in the world*. I made it up myself, actually.'

She held out a handkerchief embroidered with candy canes and holly and peppered with holes, opening it slowly to reveal two slightly squashed mince pies with stale crusts.

'It's a feast!' she said. 'One each!'

They settled down in the snow and Rinki spread the small handkerchief out as if it were a sprawling picnic blanket.

'This street corner is where Christmas trees are sold,' she said. 'It's my favourite.'

Blanche stole a glance at the alleyway behind them, where Rinki had made a tent bed with an old blanket. She thought Rinki was probably alone this Christmas too.

'Such a lovely day for a mince-pie picnic! The most glorious weather, don't you agree?' Rinki said as she handed Blanche a mince pie. 'And it is pleasure to have you both here.'

She split her mince pie in two and fed one half to Rudy, then she raised the other half in the air like an adult would raise a glass to toast an occasion.

'To Christmas!' she cheered, shoving the mince pie in her mouth.

Blanche laughed. 'To Christmas!'

They spent hours out there, lying on their backs and making snow angels and talking about all sorts of things.

Like Blanche, Rinki was an orphan who fended for herself on the streets.

'One day I'll have a family and a kitchen full of freshly baked mince pies!' Rinki said, leaping to her feet. 'I know it!'

Just then a horse pulling a gleaming green carriage turned on to their street and came trundling towards them at speed.

'CAREFUL!' Blanche cried, pulling Rinki to safety.

They watched with relief as the driver skidded on two wheels to avoid crushing their feast.

'I WISH YOU A MERRY CHRISTMAS AND MANY MINCE PIES!' Rinki called after him.

'Look at that,' Blanche said, watching the horse and carriage go. 'I'd love one of those.'

'A horse and carriage?' Rinki asked. 'Why?'

'Because everyone with a carriage has somewhere to go.' She melted back down into the snow. 'I'd like to be one of those people.'

'Well, you already have the horse,' Rinki said, nodding at Rudy. 'You're halfway there!'

Blanche grinned at the thought. 'Maybe I'll make my own with bits I find on the streets, just like your outfit!'

Rudy let out a groan at the prospect of being attached to the cart version of Rinki's outfit.

'A spectacular idea!' Rinki said. 'We can do anything – and we will. I'm going to design beautiful dresses and wear them to dances and the theatre. And I'm going to sniff out the most delicious mince pies in the world for exceptional mince-pie picnics – and you're invited, of course!'

Blanche laughed, staring adoringly at Rinki.

While all of London tucked into their Christmas dinners, outside on the corner where Christmas trees were sold, the most important friendship for the future of Christmas had taken root.

Blanche couldn't believe her luck in finding someone as strange and wonderful as Rinki. Someone who shared her mince pies, no questions asked. When she'd woken up that morning, she'd had nothing – and now she had a horse, a friend and a mysterious bauble.

'What's that?' Rinki asked, prodding the bauble in Blanche's pocket.

Blanche carefully handed it to her.

'It's colder than ice!' Rinki cried. 'But it's been in your pocket.'

Blanche nodded. 'If you think that's strange, look inside it.'

Rinki did as she was told, scrunching up her face. She moved the bauble up and down and rotated it, looking from every possible angle.

'That tree is *dancing*!' she finally screeched. 'DANCING! And with great gusto at that.'

'Where do you think that snowy world is meant to be?' Blanche whispered.

Rinki thought for a moment. 'It's somewhere much colder than London. Somewhere north of here, perhaps?'

'But do you think it's real?' Blanche said. 'It's a dancing fir tree, and trees can't dance ...'

'Not here they can't! But clearly *there* they can ... wherever *there* is.'

Blanche stared deep inside the bauble again.

'Lots of unusual things have happened to me today, Rinki, and I think it's because of the bauble.'

'Do you think the bauble is showing you your *destiny*?' Rinki said.

'You think my destiny is to become a dancing fir tree?' Blanche replied flatly. 'Excellent, I'll look forward to that.'

'You know, I'd still like you if you were a dancing tree. I could make you some fabulous decorations.'

Blanche smiled and shoved the bauble back in her pocket.

Rinki folded her handkerchief and tied it neatly

around her sleeve, so its previous owner could still see it if they happened to pass by.

'That's a lovely handkerchief,' Blanche said.

'It's my greatest find. I love the jolly bits of sparkly holly! Jolly holly!' she shouted. Then louder, 'JOLLY HOLLY!'

'JOLLY HOLLY!' Blanche joined in, their voices echoing around them. 'JOLLY HOLLY! JOLLY HOLLY!'

'Rinki,' Blanche said, lying back in the snow yet feeling warmer than she'd ever felt before. 'I have an idea.'

She reached into her pocket and pulled the gold thread free from the bauble's clasp. Carefully, she split the thread in two and wound one half around Rinki's middle finger – a little gold thread ring. She fashioned one for herself too.

'To say thank you for today, and to show we'll be friends for as long as we wear them,' Blanche said.

'It's magical!' Rinki said. 'I will never take it off!'

They stayed there until night fell and the glowing lights of Christmas began to fade. It was time for bed.

'Will you come back tomorrow?' Rinki asked.

'Of course I will. And every day after that!' Blanche said as she climbed on to Rudy's back.

Rinki smiled.

'Goodnight, Blanche! See you tomorrow!' she called.

'Goodnight, Rinki!'

Blanche waved and waved until her friend was out of sight.

After that, she sat quietly, watching the lights of London stream past to the sound of racing hooves.

For the first time in her life she had felt the magic of Christmas.

The very next day the snow began to melt, and Blanche waded excitedly through the slush with Rudy to meet her new friend.

But on the corner where Christmas trees were sold, there was nothing to be found. Not a single soul, and certainly no Rinki. In fact, there was no trace of her ever being there.

'Her things were right here,' Blanche said, choking back tears. 'Rudy, you saw her!'

Rudy spluttered an indignant yes. She wasn't going

to forget the fright Rinki had given her in a hurry.

'Leaping Christmas trees,' Blanche whispered, retracing her steps and going over every word, every moment. 'She was *right here* ... wasn't she?' Blanche waited for hours, and returned day after day to look for her friend.

But just like the snow, Rinki was gone.

FIVE YEARS LATER

Chapter 4
Blanche the Carter

Blanche Claus was dressed as a boy because she had to be.

It was the 1st of December and the snow had arrived. Winter was wrapping itself around London like a festive ribbon.

Down at the docks, carts rolled through muddy slush as workers unloaded ships. Clusters of whispering people began to arrive, sticking fast to the snow until there was a sizeable crowd. They talked excitedly of a captain and his ship. Blanche, in her usual solitary style, was far from the gossip, busily hammering at her cart.

'Finished!' she cheered, standing proudly next to Rudy. 'What do you think?'

The horse exhaled loudly and refused to look.

'Oh come on!' Blanche said, pointing to the planks of wood she had attached under each of the cart's wheels. 'It's to help us slide over the snow – our cart now works like a sleigh!'

Blanche waited for a response, but her horse was giving her nothing. When she had finished building the cart earlier that year, Rudy had responded with a similarly disgruntled noise. It had taken years to complete, and to be fair to Rudy, it was barely a cart. But it worked and it was all theirs, and now Blanche could go anywhere!

Well, anywhere she was asked to go. She had used Rudy and her cart to get a job as a carter, transporting cargo from the ships into town. But girls weren't allowed to be carters, hence the disguise.

'Girls aren't allowed to be carters,' she parroted in a silly voice to Rudy, remembering the day she was told she could never do the job. 'It's not a job for girls!'

Rudy leaned closer to Blanche, nudging her in solidarity.

Blanche cupped her hands, blowing warm air on her fingers to thaw them.

'And yet here I am,' she said. 'A rule easily broken with a big cap and trousers.'

No one suspected Blanche was a girl, and she had gained a reputation as the best carter in London – much to the annoyance of the carter boys who worked the same stretch of docks.

'Look at all these people,' Blanche said to Rudy, nodding at the crowd. 'Apparently they're here to see some fancy ship docking. Captained by a famous polar explorer—'

'Oi, Flimp!'

Blanche jumped and turned to see Whipper, the tallest of the carter boys, walking fast in her direction.

She hastily felt her cap to check that her long hair was still hidden.

'Fliiiiimp,' came more cries. This time from Cole and Sprout, Whipper's sidekicks, who were following close behind.

Flimp was what they called her. No one had ever asked her real name.

'Come any closer and I'll set Rudy on you,' Blanche growled, grabbing a grooming brush and brandishing it at them.

Whipper stifled a smirk as Rudy munched on some old rope with what remained of her teeth.

'No need to set your *terrifying* horse on me, I only want to give you a present,' he said, barging past Rudy and putting his arm around Blanche.

'A present?' Blanche said flatly.

It sounded highly unlikely, but although the carter boys had never once been kind to her, a tiny part of her wanted it to be true. It was a lonely life with only Rudy to talk to.

She let Whipper guide her towards the old stone tack hut where the carters kept their bridles and boots. It was lopsided, with mud-splashed stones and a crooked slate roof, and Blanche was never allowed inside it. The carters slept there, but not her. She still had her secret spot under the bridge.

'It's in there,' he said, nudging Blanche inside. 'You're going to love it.'

'Where?' she said, peering into the darkness. 'I can't see it.'

'Right there,' Whipper said. 'By the fireplace.'

She stepped a little further inside. It was dark without a candle and the saddles on the wall hung over her like floating ghosts ready to pounce.

There was a creak – the sound of fast boots on the old wooden floor. She reeled round, but it was too late. She caught only a quick glance of the laughing boy's face as the door slammed shut.

'NO!' she cried, racing towards it and hammering as hard as she could, furious that she'd fallen for the trick. She heard the key turn in the lock.

'LET ME OUT!' she roared. 'LET ME OUT!'

Nothing.

She crumpled on to the floor and tucked her hand into her pocket to feel the red bauble.

She still had it, and the little gold thread ring. Now it only fitted her pinky finger, but she never took it off, just in case Rinki ever came back.

Blanche thought of the corner where Christmas trees were sold and all the times she had returned to it. But although Rinki was never there, every year, without fail, she would find a dozen mince pies sitting in the same spot that she and Rinki had had their mince-pie picnic. Freshly baked, perfect and wrapped in a handkerchief.

She often wondered if she'd imagined Rinki. If perhaps she hadn't existed at all.

The clatter of hooves outside and the shouts of a substantial crew made Blanche jolt.

She lifted her head and pressed her ear to the door.

'The ship!' she cried. 'Of *course*. Their mean little trick was to get me out of the way.'

She got to her feet and rammed a determined shoulder into the door. But it was no good.

Maybe I'll let them have this one, she thought. She hadn't been that interested in the fancy ship anyway, plus a rich captain was no guarantee of a good fee.

'JOLLY HOLLY!' came a cry from outside, making Blanche freeze. 'JOLLY HOLLY! JOLLY HOLLY!'

The words echoed through her mind, lifting her up and all the way back to that empty London street all those Christmases ago. *JOLLY HOLLY!* she could hear Rinki cheer. *JOLLY HOLLY! JOLLY HOLLY!*

Was she out there?

She jumped to her feet. She had to get out! But it was

impossible – the door wouldn't budge and there were no windows, only a fireplace and horse brushes and bridles.

Blanche's eyes grew wide as she remembered the trick she would use to exit the orphanages.

'Just like old times!' she said confidently, striding over to the fireplace and sticking her head inside the chimney. She grabbed hold of one of the wobbly stones, shaking it to test how sturdy it was. Then she reached as high as she could and began to haul herself up, clawing her way through the thick cobwebs and soot, up and up until her head popped out of the top of the chimney.

She scanned the crowds, desperately hoping to glimpse her friend. It took her a moment to remember to breathe.

The ship in the dock did indeed look particularly grand, but what Blanche saw made her slump with disappointment.

Its large bow was decorated with carvings of holly.

The ship was called the *Jolly Holly*, and the people outside were shouting its name.

It was nothing to do with Rinki at all.

The ship's crew in vivid green waistcoats lowered sails and scrubbed the deck, and in the middle of the commotion stood a man as grand as the ship. He had the beard of an explorer, bushy and wild, and little round glasses that looked like they held the wisdom of the world. His attention was on the small iron box he was holding. Blanche was wondering why it was so interesting, when he looked up and spotted her sticking out of the chimney. She considered ducking, but instead went for an awkward wave. His stern face cracked a smile and he tipped his hat at her.

An adventurer can always spot another.

Blanche didn't want to miss a chance to see him up close. She heaved herself out of the chimney and on to the roof, sliding on the frosty slates as if she were on skis. She picked up speed – too much speed! – and rolled straight off, disappearing into a pile of freshly shovelled snow. When she emerged, sooty but in one piece, Rudy was standing over her with the reins in her mouth.

'Tally-ho,' Blanche whispered with a grin.

Next to the gangplank of the *Jolly Holly* the carter boys were parading up and down with their horses and carts, bumping into each other in their attempts to look as impressive as possible.

'Very good, very good,' the captain said wearily as the boys skidded back and forth. 'I don't really care which of you it is, as long as you're fast. It doesn't really mat—'

He broke off as his eyes shifted to the carter who had just arrived.

'You,' he said, pointing at Blanche and her makeshift sleigh. 'You'll be the quickest with that thing.'

The boys whipped round.

'NOT FLIMP!' Whipper cried.

'He was locked up!' Cole hissed. 'I've had the key on me the whole time!'

Sprout gawped at the locked door. 'How'd you get out?'

'Three guesses, geniuses,' Blanche said as she trotted past in a cloud of soot. 'Now, Captain, where is your cargo?'

She looked to the piles of trunks and barrels, but the captain held up the small box, glancing over his shoulder as if he expected company.

'Just this,' he said.

'Just that? Are you sure, Captain … ?'

'Garland,' he said distantly, as if his mind were on something else. 'I'm sorry, what was I saying? Oh, my name is Captain Garland. And you are Flimp, I believe?'

'It's a cruel nickname,' Blanche explained. 'But it has unfortunately stuck.'

'It means pickpocket!' Cole shouted. 'Because Flimp's always stealing our jobs!'

'Case. In. Point,' Whipper said with a bitter wave in her direction.

Blanche ignored them and climbed back on to the cart. She placed the box carefully beside her. The lid was covered in iron stars and three locks kept it closed, each keyhole shaped like an intricate snowflake. They would need the most elaborate set of keys. She wondered what would require such special security.

'Bet Flimp gets more shillings from that captain than we've got all year,' Sprout said. He dismounted and stormed towards the tack hut. 'I'll never be rich at this rate!'

'Please take extra special care,' Captain Garland said, looking past Blanche to two strange men dressed in black suits lurking among the crowd. They stood deathly still and wore their hats so low it was impossible to see their faces. But even so, the ice-cold tickle on the back of Blanche's neck made her sure they were staring at her.

'Here,' Captain Garland said with haste, and he pressed a heavy bag of coins into her hand. It was a far heftier fee than was required for such a seemingly small job. 'Take the box to my home at 6 Stratton Street as quickly as you can, and don't stop for anything or anyone, you hear?'

Blanche nodded as she gathered up the reins and readied herself. She looked down at the box to check it was secure …

And that was when she was sure she saw it move.

'Straight to Stratton Street,' Captain Garland said, his voice growing louder.

The crowd began to shriek, and Blanche turned in alarm to see a perfect path was being carved straight to her as people fell right and left and the strange men walked right over them. They were coming for her.

'Go!' Captain Garland said. 'And whatever you do, *don't stop.*'

Chapter 5

The Cane with a Thousand Eyes

Blanche charged through the snowy streets of London in the pink dusk light.

No one knew the streets like her, and no one could move a horse and cart like her either. She kept glancing back, checking for the strange men, but it seemed she had lost them straight out of the docks. She pulled gently on the reins and Rudy took a sharp left down a crowded cobbled alleyway.

'NOT YOU AGAIN!' came a shout from a man washing underpants in the gutter. 'YOU CAN'T FIT DOWN HERE!'

Blanche grabbed the limp string of the man's washing line, pulling it taut for him as they skidded past.

'SHOW OFF!' he yelled.

Rudy neighed in delight as they shot out of an alleyway by Green Park and tore across the open parkland. For as far as Blanche could see, children were building snowmen and throwing snowballs and making impossibly long lines of snow angels.

Ugh, snowmen, she thought. *That means Christmas.*

Since the Christmas with Rinki, she'd stopped counting down the seconds until it was over and replaced it with a more torturous tradition that made her hate it just as much. Now, she would sit and have a mince-pie picnic alone, with the strangely perfect mince pies that she found at the spot where she'd met Rinki. And then she would ugly cry for hours.

When they reached Piccadilly there was no choice but to stop. Horses and the sort of fancy carriages only found in the nice parts of town rumbled past, blocking the way across to Stratton Street. Blanche took the opportunity to stand up and get a better look at the place Captain Garland called home.

'Looks as fancy as his ship,' she said, craning her neck to see. 'Rudy, look at those houses – four storeys tall and filled with roaring fires, I bet!'

The horse responded by lurching forward.

'RUDY!' Blanche cried. 'The *traffic*.'

It wasn't like Rudy to act up, but act up she did – first throwing her head in the air, then bouncing sideways. Blanche was so focused on steadying her, it took a moment to see the hands reaching for the box. In that moment, panic engulfed her and all of London began to swirl out of her control.

'THAT BELONGS TO CAPTAIN GARLAND!' she cried, desperately hauling herself across the cart so her whole body was on top of the box. A spindly hand writhed underneath her, tightening its grip on its prize.

'Give us the box,' one of the strange men whispered.

'She's really heavy,' squeaked the other. 'It's hurting my hand.' He got a prod in the ribs for that and it allowed Blanche a second of relief to slip the box out from under her.

'Ha! TOO SLOW!' she said, holding it triumphantly in the air.

The strange men slowly looked up at her, revealing what was under their hats. She recoiled in horror at what was there – or rather what *wasn't*. There was no neck, no face, no head. Nothing but snow-filled air.

She gasped and the box fell to her feet with a clang.

'Told you the headless thing would come in handy,' one whispered to the other.

'IS THIS FILTHY CHILD CAUSING TROUBLE?' came a booming voice.

Blanche turned to see a man standing behind her. He was tall and furious-looking, with a clipped black beard as dark as his beady eyes. But it was his cane that scared Blanche the most. It was as sinister as a cane could be, carved with a thousand eyes that all stared in her direction. At the top it split, spiking into two menacing horns.

'Well?' he said, stabbing the snow with his cane and making Blanche jump. 'I can only assume this hideous scrounger of a child is causing you bother, gentlemen. Has it stolen from you? They always steal.'

Blanche shakily bent down and scooped up the box, hugging it close to her chest.

'No,' she said bravely. 'The men with NO FACES were trying to steal from *me*.'

The strange men began talking fast in hushed whispers only Blanche could hear.

'I told you it was too much!'

'I think it's better to be sinister and intimidating.'

'I think being *headless* draws a little too much attention!'

The man stabbed the snow with his cane again and locked eyes with Blanche. His look was enough to make her shiver.

'NO FACES?' he finally said, followed by a hollow laugh. 'Making a mockery of respectable folk, are you? You're stealing from these two men in fine hats and we all know it. Did you threaten them with violence?'

Blanche's mouth fell open to protest, but she couldn't find the words she needed.

'I know your sort, you vile creature. Always taking advantage of hard-working people. Now, gentlemen,' he said a little more softly, turning his attention to the strange men. 'Tell me what happen—'

He stopped.

The strange men had vanished.

'Where the devil are they?' he snapped, ducking under the cart to see if they were hiding.

'Oh wonderful, I think you scared the criminals off,' Blanche said, putting on a high and haughty voice. 'Thank you *very much*.'

She gathered up the reins and stuck her nose in the air. There was a perfect break in the traffic and she and Rudy trotted off smugly towards Stratton Street.

Stratton Street was picture perfect that evening. Fresh snow coated the cobbles and Blanche watched as her breath frosted and floated away in the glow of candle-light from welcoming windows.

'Imagine living here,' she whispered to Rudy. 'It's magical.'

They pulled up outside number 6, the grandest house of them all. In the bay window at the front, servants were struggling to move a Christmas tree into place.

One was mouthing left and the other was gesturing right and the one in the middle didn't seem to know what to think. They stopped when they spotted Blanche with the iron box in her hands.

She waved and pointed towards the alleyway to the back of the house, where she would be expected to drop it off.

'I've got a delivery,' she mouthed up to them.

But the servants didn't move. They were frozen, their eyes trained on the box.

'What is it about this box?' Blanche whispered to Rudy as she jumped off the cart, her boots slipping on the icy ground. The servants still hadn't moved.

'Hello?' she tried again, waving at them.

Still no movement.

Blanche began jumping up and down. 'CAN YOU SEE ME? HELLO?'

Rudy neighed.

'Hang on, Rudy,' Blanche said.

The box began to shake. Rudy began kicking snow. Blanche felt the panic rising in her, but she dared to look anyway.

The suited men were striding up the street.

'HELLO! EMERGENCY! BOX THEFT IN PROGRESS!' she shouted, racing up the steps and hammering hard on the door.

The men were only fifty yards away now. The servants had gone from the window.

'I HAVE AN IMPORTANT DELIVERY FOR CAPTAIN GARLAND! SOMEONE LET ME IN!

'SOMEONE!

'LET!

'ME!

'IN!'

The door whipped open and, as though something had frightened them, the suited men backed away into the shadows.

Blanche stared at the girl who had answered her plea, unable to believe her eyes. She was older now, and just like Blanche she had moved the little gold thread ring to her pinky finger.

'Rinki?' Blanche managed to whisper as the girl leaped barefoot into the snow and hugged her tightly.

'IT'S YOU! IT'S BLANCHE CLAUS!'

Chapter 6
The Red Suit

Rinki was no longer wearing lost and found bits of Christmas. Instead, she wore a gorgeous silk dress, puffed and purple, with a silver ribbon in her hair.

'I've been looking for you for years, I worried the worst had happened!' Rinki said, looking Blanche up and down to check she was all right. 'I went back to the corner where Christmas trees are sold every year to wait for you. I searched under bridges, because you said that's where you slept. And every year, I left mince pies on the corner where Christmas trees are sol—'

'I found them!' Blanche interrupted. 'I found them every year!'

'Oh!' Rinki said, clasping her hands together with delight. 'So at least you had magical mince-pie picnics, even if it was without me?'

Blanche nodded slowly as memories of her snot-crying into pastry flashed through her mind. 'Er, magical ... yes.'

'Come inside so I can get a better look at you! You've got so much taller – and you've cut your hair!' Rinki said, nodding at Blanche's cap.

'Oh, no,' Blanche said, taking it off and letting her long white hair tumble out. 'I just have to hide it – girls aren't allowed to be carters, you see.'

Rinki growled in disapproval as she guided Blanche down the hallway and into the study.

'But you did it,' Rinki said, beaming at her friend. 'You got your carriage. I bet you're the best carter in London.'

Blanche looked down at her boots bashfully. 'Well ...'

'Knew it,' Rinki said.

'But what happened to you?' Blanche asked. 'Why

47

didn't you come and find me that Christmas?'

'Oh, Blanche. I'm so sorry. The day after Christmas, the day we arranged to meet, I was found by Captain Garland and Teddy – they adopted me, and I've lived here ever since.'

Blanche looked around the study, with its plum-painted walls half hidden by sketches and ribbons and scraps of fabric tacked in place. The room was full of mannequins sporting elaborate dresses like the one Rinki was wearing, along with capes and hats and shoes, all half-made.

'You know, I did always scribble a note on the handkerchief I wrapped the mince pies in,' Rinki said. 'Did you never see them?'

Memories of aggressively blowing her nose into handkerchiefs crashed into Blanche's mind.

'Um … no … I never saw the notes,' she said awkwardly.

'Five wasted years – we must make up for it!' Rinki said as she plonked herself down in one of the armchairs by the fire. 'I talk about you every day, but because we never found you, everyone thinks I made you up.'

Blanche gently placed the box on the table. In all the excitement of being reunited with Rinki she had forgotten she was still holding it.

'I can't believe you're here – Blanche Claus, standing right in front of me. It's like the best kind of dream!'

She turned and looked out of the window.

'And Rudy too! She hasn't aged a bit!'

'Oh, Rudy was too old to get any older,' Blanche said, sounding distracted.

A beautiful red suit with a glistening red cape had caught her eye.

It hung quietly on the mannequin in the corner, in the shadows of the other outfits. Blanche slowly ran her hand over it.

'Lovely, isn't it?' Rinki said. 'Teddy's been trying to finish that one for ages. He thinks it needs something extra though, but he can't decide what.'

There was a gasp at the door and a handsome man with a mop of gingerbread-coloured hair stepped into the room. He'd teamed his sparkling gold jacket with orange trousers and a pair of pink slippers with toy soldiers embroidered on them. Blanche was sure he was the best-dressed man she had ever seen.

'*That* is what it needs,' he said, striding over to Blanche and holding up her long white hair to the edge of the suit. 'A beautiful snow-white trim!'

'Teddy,' Rinki said excitedly. 'This is Blanche Claus!'

He held his hand to his heart.

'Oh, my dear Blanche! We thought you were completely made up!' He shook Blanche's hand enthusiastically. 'It is an honour to meet you. Truly, the biggest honour!'

'And it's an honour to meet you,' Blanche said. 'I'm glad Rinki found such a lovely home.'

'And I'm glad we found her,' he said. 'When I saw her wearing that wrapping-paper skirt and holding my lost Christmas handkerchief, I knew our stories were meant to collide.'

'Teddy says that in life you always find your people,' Rinki said.

'Case in point!' he said, and Blanche was sure she could see his lip tremble. 'You two have found each other again. Oh, it's wonderful!' He eyed her outfit. 'And your outfit is … you're a—'

'A carter,' Blanche replied.

'She has to pretend to be a boy, because girls aren't allowed to be carters,' Rinki said. 'Isn't that awful?'

Teddy rolled his eyes. 'Sometimes the world makes no sense.'

'Blanche was delivering the box,' Rinki said to him.

'Well, at least something good has come from having that thing,' Teddy groaned.

'It must mean Jolly is on his way,' Rinki said as she wiped the window with her cuff to get a better view of the street. 'Can't see him yet.'

'Jolly is what Rinki calls Captain Garland,' Teddy said with a smile. 'His real name is Gadin. He's wonderfully serious and Jolly doesn't suit him at all, which is why I adore the nickname.'

'Do you sail ships too?' Blanche asked Teddy excitedly.

'Blanche, you wouldn't catch me dead on a ship!' Teddy said. 'I get seasick walking past the fishmonger's. No, I prefer making dresses.'

'Teddy funds Jolly's expeditions with his designs. You wouldn't *believe* what some of his dresses sell for!' Rinki said. 'Everyone is mad for them. Well, everyone except horrible Mr Krampus next door, who doesn't like anything or anyone.'

Blanche laughed. 'I suppose you can't please everyone.'

She looked at the outfits dotted everywhere around the room.

'So these are all yours,' she said. 'Your designs are beautiful.'

'Teddy's the head of the London Costume Society,' Rinki explained, making her father blush. 'He makes the best party outfits in the world.'

'Don't tell anyone,' he whispered, 'but I'm making Queen Victoria's Christmas ball dress.'

'She comes here for secret fittings,' Rinki said.

'Wow,' Blanche said. 'The *Queen*.'

Rinki slumped back in the chair and scrunched up her face.

'She has good taste in dressmakers, and that's about it.'

Teddy nodded and glanced out of the window. 'The horse is here! Rinki has told us so much about her. Rudy, I believe?'

'Yes, that's Rudy,' Blanche said proudly. She noticed Rudy was scratching her back against a lamp post. 'She's the best horse in London, and I'd say the whole world too, if I was to hazard a guess.'

She hesitated.

'My carter fee normally includes a carrot for her, but I didn't have a moment to ask Captain Garland for it.'

Teddy smiled. 'Well,' he said, 'I'm going to take Rudy round to the stables, where it's nice and warm and she can have a *pile* of fresh carrots. That'll give you two some time to catch up.'

He made for the door. 'White trim. Red suit. Perfection!'

'Goodbye, Teddy,' Blanche said with a wave. 'It was lovely to meet you.'

Teddy stopped dead in his tracks. 'Oh no, never goodbye! I hate that word. You will come and see us again very soon, won't you?'

Blanche assured him that she would, and he left the room, whistling as he went.

Rinki, meanwhile, had begun trying to prise the box open.

'Odd, isn't it?' she said. 'None of the servants will go anywhere near it.'

'I think that's because there are some really scary men looking for it,' Blanche said. 'Do you see those strange figures out there lurking in the shadows?'

Rinki looked.

'So they're back, are they?'

'You mean you know about them?' Blanche said. 'They followed me all the way here from the docks.'

'I can believe it,' Rinki said. 'I've seen them before, but they don't scare me.'

Blanche decided not to mention they might be headless.

'What's in the box that they want so badly?'

Rinki shrugged. 'I don't know. Jolly has the keys, but he won't open it. He brought it home one day, and whenever he leaves it goes with him, and when he returns it comes back to us, and so do the strange

men. They seem to only go for the box when it's outside the house.'

Blanche peered out across the snowy street. 'I'd love to know what's inside.'

'Me too,' Rinki said, looking around and lowering her voice to a whisper. 'I'm sure I once saw it move.'

'I saw it move too!' Blanche cried.

'It must be something Jolly discovered on one of his expeditions – but he says it's a secret and it needs to be returned to where it came from. He told me it's better that only he knows, in case it falls into the wrong hands. He's very secretive about it,' Rinki explained. 'Which is odd because he usually tells me everything …'

She trailed off, as though a thought had just occurred to her. 'Blanche, do you still have your bauble?'

Blanche took it from her pocket. 'I still have it. You can still see the dancing Christmas tree.'

They both held it tight, Rinki's hands wrapped around Blanche's.

'Jolly once told me about a place he believes exists somewhere, hidden by magic and wrapped in snow. A lot like the place inside your bauble.'

'You mean it might truly be real?' Blanche said hopefully.

As she said it, it seemed as though the snow began to fall faster outside the window, as if the weather were as excited as she was at the thought. She looked to the red suit in the corner of the room, and she had the strangest feeling.

'Ah, heavy snow!' Rinki said, interrupting Blanche's thoughts. 'You know what that means?'

'What does it mean?'

'Time for a mince-pie picnic!'

Chapter 7

Mince Pies and Rooftops and What Could Be

In the kitchen, Blanche helped tip a tray of mince pies into Rinki's upturned skirt – despite the servants' cries to use a plate.

'Mince-pie picnics don't need plates!' Rinki declared as they climbed the stairs.

Blanche stopped in the doorway to Rinki's room, staring at the roaring flames in the fireplace at the end of her bed. She tried to imagine what it would be like to sleep on a bed with plump pillows and feel heat at her feet.

Rinki's room was full of trinkets and toys. Books filled the bookcases and tumbled out from under her bed, and she grabbed a tall one to wedge the window open.

'This way,' she said, throwing a leg over the edge of the sill. She stopped and stuck her tongue out to catch the snow. 'Ah yes, just as I suspected – perfect mince-pie picnic snow! Couldn't be better!'

Blanche followed Rinki outside, pulling herself up on to the roof and joining her friend by the chimney. The wind whistled in her ears and Blanche breathed in the icy air. It was dark now and all of London twinkled. She looked out across the city, unable to believe she and Rinki were reunited at last.

'For tradition's sake,' Rinki said, and carefully placed a handkerchief down – the same one she'd had before, with the holes and the holly and the candy canes. The mince pies were different though, piping hot and plentiful. She lined them up, then split one in half and raised it in the air.

'Cheers!'

'Cheers!' Blanche said, tapping her half against Rinki's. She paused before the mince pie hit her lips. 'Wait!'

The handkerchief had reminded her of something.

'Did you name Captain Garland's ship the *Jolly Holly*?'

Rinki grinned. 'That was all me.'

'When I heard everyone at the docks shouting "Jolly Holly", I hoped it was something to do with you.'

They sat in silence for a moment, concentrating on their mince pies.

'You must be so happy living here,' Blanche said.

'I am.' Rinki shoved an entire mince pie in her mouth in a way only a mince-pie picnic expert could. 'But what about you? Where do you live now?'

'Still under my old bridge,' Blanche said. 'But now I make enough money to feed Rudy well. And one day I'll find a home just like you did.'

'But Blanche!' Rinki cried. 'You can't live under a bridge. You should come and live here – there's plenty of room.'

Blanche felt overwhelmed at the thought. 'Here? With you?'

'Yes!' Rinki cried. 'It's perfect. And you won't have to be a carter – instead you'd be driven around in a lovely carriage, whisked away to balls to dance the night away!'

'But,' Blanche said as a dusting of doubt settled over the idea, 'I actually quite like being a carter. And … well, I suppose the more I think about it, coming here would be living your life. And as wonderful as it sounds, and as magnificent as Captain Garland and Teddy are, they're your family, not mine.'

'No,' Rinki said, shaking her head. 'You must. I won't have it any other way.'

'If I'm here living this life – *your* life – then my own life, my people, won't ever find me.'

Hearing Teddy's words repeated back to her made Rinki stop arguing.

'Well, just remember there's a place here for you,' Rinki said, biting into another mince pie. 'I hate that you have to pretend to be a boy though.'

'*Me too*,' Blanche said.

'One day things will be different,' Rinki said. 'One day the world will imagine more of girls. We'll make sure of it!'

'We could change the world if only they'd let us,'

Blanche said, lying back in the snow.

'*Let us?*' Rinki scoffed. 'We don't have to ask permission. I like that you became a carter – it was something you wanted to do and so you did it. You're wonderful! I knew it the day we met.'

She flopped down next to Blanche and stared up at the sky.

'What would you do, if you could do anything in the world? Wildest dreams stuff.'

Blanche curled her hand around the bauble in her pocket. She'd thought about it many times before and knew exactly what she was going to say.

'Do you remember I told you about the old lady – the one who gave me the bauble … ?'

'Yes.' Rinki nodded.

'Well, that day changed my life. And I've often wondered if I could do the same for someone else. I think if I could do it, I'd give every child in the world a present on Christmas Day.'

Rinki turned to her and beamed.

'That would be magical!'

'Exactly.' Blanche nodded. 'I would like them to wake

up to a little present that reminds them that the world *is* magical. That there are adventures out there waiting for them.'

Rinki squeezed Blanche's hand tightly.

'And who knows, maybe I could give a gift to a child who felt alone just like we did. And it would show them that they're not alone, that friends *will* find them, just like the present found them on Christmas Day.'

'I love that idea,' Rinki said wistfully.

Blanche held up her mince pie. She was about to change the subject and compliment the cook's baking when Rinki sat bolt upright.

'Let's do it. If anyone can do it, it's us!'

'Do what?' Blanche asked.

'Give a gift to every child in the world on Christmas Day!'

Blanche laughed. 'It's impossible! You said if I could do *anything*. I didn't mean it was something we actually *could* do.'

But Rinki's face was serious and businesslike. 'You'll need to be able to get around the world. Is Rudy up to it?'

'I think she'd have to fly!' Blanche joked.

Rinki smiled and with her finger scored something off an imaginary list in the air. 'Flying horse and cart … Next? How do we get into the houses? I suppose we could just knock.'

'It's a bit ordinary though, isn't it? Like the postman. I want it to be magical. Imagine if there was a present *just there* when they woke up!'

'We could deliver them while they sleep,' Rinki suggested.

'But how?' Blanche asked.

They sat silently in the snow, thinking hard.

'What about throwing them through a window?' Rinki said.

'Not safe enough!' Blanche said. 'We might smack someone right in the face – that's the *opposite* of Christmas.'

She got to her feet and began pacing the roof. She stopped, remembering her trick.

'We could climb down the chimney!'

'PERFECTION!' Rinki scored another item off her imaginary list. 'Another thing sorted. Well done, Blanche!'

Blanche stared up at the sky and smiled. 'Imagine what the world would think of girls if they saw us flying through the sky. It could change everything.'

'One day we'll write the stories, and make the rules,' Rinki said. 'One day we *will* change the world.'

'And we won't have to be disguised as boys to do it,' Blanche said with a satisfied smile.

The snow began to fall faster and thicker, in torn tufts of glistening white until everything from their boots to their eyelashes was covered.

Blanche looked out across the rooftops at the hundreds of chimneys of every shape and size.

I wonder, she thought.

Chapter 8

Let Your Heart Be Light

After the mince-pie picnic, Blanche and Rinki were practically inseparable.

As soon as Blanche finished a shift at the docks, she'd ride across town to Stratton Street to see her friend, while the servants groomed Rudy to perfection and fed her a bucket of carrots. Soon the residents of Stratton Street came to expect the battered cart's arrival outside the Garlands' home. Rinki, Teddy and Captain Garland always tried to persuade Blanche to stay with them, but she was determined to forge her own path.

'You're stubborn,' Rinki said, prodding Blanche with a carrot. 'She's just like you, Jolly, a hardened adventurer.'

The neighbours would have gossiped about the carter's daily visits if they hadn't been distracted by the two strange men in suits, who stood outside day and night, sleet and snow.

The odd thing was that whenever any of the neighbours decided to do something about them, they would march to their front doors and then completely forget why they were going out in the first place. It was as if the strange men were even stranger than they all suspected.

On the 2nd of December, Blanche and Rinki painted Christmas cards by firelight, while Captain Garland mapped his next voyage and Teddy stitched a snow-white trim on the red suit.

On the 3rd of December, they caught falling snowflakes on their tongues and threw snowballs at the fancy carriages. That night Rinki handed Blanche a letter. 'Don't open it until you get home. Promise?'

When Blanche arrived, she found a little stone hut had been built under the bridge and decorated with red glass baubles. She ripped open Rinki's letter.

It's called Christmas Lodge.

Inside was a bed with plump pillows, a tiny fireplace with flames roaring in its hearth, and a tray of mince pies. Teddy had sewn some pretty green curtains for the windows and a soft purple rug covered the floor.

Blanche stood in the doorway, unable to believe her eyes.

'Christmas Lodge,' she whispered with a smile.

On the 4th of December, they lay in thick snow and made snow angels. Blanche could sense the lonely feeling she knew so well melting away. It was hard to imagine she'd ever felt such a thing at all.

'Come on, Blanche!' Rinki shouted. She'd made it almost halfway across the park without Blanche even noticing. 'I want to show you my favourite statue!'

Soon they stopped at the base of a towering sculpture of a woman, her arms raised high at the front of a horse-drawn chariot.

'Who is she?' Blanche whispered in awe.

'Boudicca,' Rinki said. 'She's the woman who

conquered London. When the Romans invaded, they tried to take everything from her, so she fought them and won.'

'And who are *they*?' Blanche could see two other figures in the back of the chariot.

'Her daughters,' Rinki said. 'It's a new statue, but an old story. I hate how people talk as if women have never achieved anything, as though we're all meek and live in the background of great stories. It's never, ever been true. We've always done brave and brilliant things, and this statue shows just one of them.'

Blanche stared up at it, the snowflakes stinging her cheeks.

'She reminds me of you,' Rinki said, before skipping off through the snow, whistling a Christmas tune.

Blanche looked closely at the fierce woman in her chariot, and for the first time in her life she saw herself.

On the 5th of December, they ran into the Garlands' neighbour Mr Krampus. Their stories entwined from here on, like the messiest of Christmas wreaths. And it is here that Blanche's story takes a dark turn.

Chapter 9
Mr Krampus

Mr Krampus could at best be described as a humbug and at worst a devil.

He was impossible to forget, and as soon as Blanche saw the man striding up Stratton Street with his menacing cane, she knew exactly where she had seen him before, though his name still remained a mystery.

'Oh, him. That's Mr Krampus,' Rinki said gravely. She held out a cup of hot chocolate for Blanche. 'Our dreadful neighbour.'

'That's *your neighbour*? He's the man I was telling you about – the one who was horrible to me the night I delivered the box.'

'I wouldn't worry too much,' Rinki said. 'He's horrible to everyone.'

Blanche watched from the window as he walked in zigzags through the snow, deliberately barging into as many people as possible. 'He gives me the shivers. That cane. It's—'

'Rumour has it the cane is carved with the eyes of his enemies – each one dead and trapped forever.' Rinki held out a jug. 'Cream?'

Blanche shot her a bewildered look.

'It's not true, obviously. It's just … what people say.'

He halted outside number 6 and ripped some mistletoe from the lamp post, stamping on it violently until it was no more than mush.

'He's not some other-world beast, he's just a man. An angry one. You know he owns *The Watcher* newspaper?' Rinki went on. 'He's always looking for stories that other newspapers don't know about, so everyone will buy his instead. He's found that the best way to get his stories is just to make them up.'

'He can do that?' Blanche asked.

'Of course. He owns the newspaper!' Rinki said. 'He

can write anything he wants. Apparently the newspaper thing is why he hates Christmas. No newspapers are published on Christmas Day, and he sees the whole thing as a massive kick in the wallet.'

Blanche turned to the window once more. But this time, Mr Krampus was staring back at her.

'He saw me!' she cried, dropping fast and curling up into a ball. 'He *definitely* saw me.'

Blanche watched Rinki back into the corner of the room, and she knew then that Rinki's attempts to play down sinister Mr Krampus had been for her benefit. Underneath it all, Rinki was just as scared of him as she was.

They stood in terrified silence, which was broken moments later by a loud bang at the door.

Blanche's heart was beating in her mouth. Rinki grabbed her arm and they raced out into the hallway, just as Cook came wafting through the kitchen door, smelling like freshly baked mince pies.

'Don't answer it,' Rinki whispered, as she and Blanche plastered themselves against the door.

'It's *Mr Krampus*,' Blanche mouthed.

71

Cook wrinkled her nose in disgust and began tiptoe-ing back to the kitchen.

'I KNOW YOU'RE IN THERE!' he shouted. 'I SAW YOU SPYING AT THE WINDOW!'

Cook sighed heavily and turned on her heel. 'Well, now I have no choice but to answer it!' She trudged over to the door, which was now rattling on its hinges Mr Krampus was knocking so hard.

Blanche and Rinki dived behind the reams of ribbons that decorated the stairs.

'He knows it's me,' Blanche fretted. 'He's come to get me.'

Cook calmly opened the door and stared at the spot where Mr Krampus had been hitting it. And then she took a deep breath.

'NO!' Mr Krampus shouted, waggling a finger in her face. 'NOT AGAIN—'

'Watch this,' Rinki said, and Cook began to scream.

She was screaming something about jingling bells, but Blanche couldn't quite make it out.

'CAPTAIN GARLAND!' Mr Krampus roared, cover-ing his ears. 'YOUR COOK IS BROKEN AGAIN!'

'It's Cook's way of dealing with Mr Krampus,' Rinki explained. 'He was very cruel to one of her friends, and so she does this whenever she's near him now. It's a protest of sorts.'

Mr Krampus shoved Cook to the side and marched towards the staircase. He was close enough for Blanche to smell his scent – like putrid liquorice and steel. He slammed his cane down, making them both jump out from behind the ribbons.

'FETCH CAPTAIN GARLAND,' he growled at Rinki, overlooking Blanche completely.

Blanche stood frozen on the spot, her heart drumming in her ears.

'And who are you?' he snapped.

'No one,' Blanche said quietly. Her voice was shaking.

He turned back to Rinki.

'DID YOU NOT HEAR ME, GIRL? CAPTAIN GARLAND – NOW!'

'I don't take orders from anyone,' Rinki said, standing tall, but Blanche could see her hands, neatly clasped behind her back, were trembling.

Cook seemed to be on to the chorus of her

screaming jingly bell song now, and had introduced hand gestures.

Mr Krampus paused and stared blankly ahead, as if suddenly distracted by a thought. He snapped back to Blanche, making her wince.

'You look familiar. Have we met?'

Luckily for Blanche, Teddy came down the stairs just in time.

'Ah, Mr Krampus,' he said in a friendly voice that Blanche could tell was entirely forced. 'Have you finally realised I'm a genius and come for a bespoke outfit?'

'Haven't you found a way to turn that woman off?' Mr Krampus spat.

At a look from Teddy, Cook nodded and made her way back to the kitchen, still screaming. She winked at Blanche before closing the door with a bang.

'I can still hear her,' Mr Krampus groaned. 'What's she screaming about bells for?'

Teddy opened his mouth to speak, but stopped when he realised he had no good answer.

'And this one,' he said, prodding Rinki in the ribs, 'hasn't been brought up properly at all.'

Teddy jumped the remainder of the stairs and stood protectively in front of Rinki and Blanche.

'Would you like something with a bit of colour, Mr Krampus? A nice tangerine orange would look wonderful with those black eyes of yours! Maybe a silk, or a taffeta. Would you consider a bow tie?'

'I'm here,' Mr Krampus said, somewhat thrown by the screaming from the kitchen and the myriad outfit suggestions, 'because there is a mangy old horse and cart that's been lingering outside your house lately, and it needs to vanish.'

'Her name is Rudy,' Teddy said. 'And the cart ... Does the cart have a name, Blanche?'

'No,' Blanche said.

'I don't care if it has a name!' Mr Krampus said, his voice growing hysterical. 'This is one of the most expensive streets in London!'

'Aren't you full of facts! Horse outside. Street expensive. Teddy's designs are works of genius—'

'I did not say that last bit.'

Teddy laughed, then his face grew serious. 'Well, all fun aside, I'm afraid, Mr Krampus, there are no rules

about what the horses and carts of Stratton Street must look like. They belong to a special and much-loved guest of ours, and so they are here to stay.'

Blanche beamed up at Teddy.

'It's an eyesore!' Mr Krampus protested. 'Riddled with disease! A danger to society!'

Blanche stepped forward to defend Rudy, but Teddy held out his arm to stop her.

'I do love a danger to society,' he said, clearly enjoying himself. 'Goodness, you've made me like the horse even more. I might throw a party in its honour – we could have a horseshoe-shaped cake and neigh instead of shouting cheers!'

'Just get rid of it!' Mr Krampus bellowed. 'I have no time for your eccentricities. If I ever see that horse and cart posing a danger around here again, I will have it removed! I hear the glue factories make fast work of old horses.'

'Take that back at once, you beast!' Blanche shouted.

Mr Krampus bared his teeth at her.

'You won't be able to stop me!' he said, waving his cane threateningly in her face. He gasped. 'I know you! I didn't recognise you without your cap. You're the carter who I caught robbing two fine gentlemen.' He turned back to Teddy. 'I stopped the brat committing a crime. A real menace to society, that one.'

'I very much doubt that,' Teddy said, putting his arm around Blanche.

A smile crept over Mr Krampus's face when he realised something else. 'And you're a *girl*!'

'Mr Krampus, leave the girl alo—' Teddy tried to interject, but the man was on a roll.

'Girls aren't allowed to be carters.' He lifted the cane and ran its horns through Blanche's long hair.

Rinki hit his cane away. 'Well, they should be, because she's the best there is.'

'And I suppose you approve of this?' Mr Krampus said, turning to Teddy. 'This blatant disregard for the rules?'

Teddy shrugged. 'I can't see a problem,' he said, as the sound of Cook screaming was joined by deliberately clattered pans.

'I'm not sure my newspaper readers would agree,' he said, smiling nastily. 'There are conventions about how

women should dress. The jobs that they should do. HOW THEY OUGHT TO BEHAVE.'

'Now, Mr Krampus,' said Teddy, looking worried for the first time. 'I'm sure this can be sorted out amicably.'

'Well, you just see that it is.' Mr Krampus shot him a deadly look. 'And for heaven's sake, stop that mad woman in your kitchen screaming!'

'She'll stop when you leave,' Rinki said.

Mr Krampus turned his beady eyes on her. 'I can see I'm going to have to do something about you,' he said menacingly.

'Now, now,' Teddy said gently, trying to calm the situation. 'Can I make you a peace offering? There are dozens of the best mince pies in London down in the kitchen and—'

'HE'S NOT GETTING ANYWHERE NEAR MY MINCE PIES,' came a guttural roar from the kitchen before the screaming recommenced.

There was a moment of awkward silence.

Blanche tried to hold in a snigger but it came bursting from her in a great splutter.

Mr Krampus narrowed his eyes. 'I don't know what

you think is so funny, *girl*. If the other carters found out your little secret, you'd never work again. What a pity. And that's what'll happen unless you take that mangy horse and cart away and never come back.'

Blanche locked eyes with Mr Krampus. She refused to look away, even though every inch of her was shaking.

The horrible man wrapped his hand tightly around the cane until his fingers cracked. He stared at each of them in turn before he took his leave.

'The world would be a better place without the likes of you lot in it!' he spat as he threw open the door.

Blanche watched as Rinki marched furiously after him, grabbing one of her elaborate feather hats from the hatstand as she went.

'Goodbye, Mr Krampus,' she said. 'Don't forget your hat.'

And with that, she shoved it on his head and closed the door behind him.

The sound of hysterical laughter erupted outside.

'MR KRAMPUS! THAT'S AN EXCITING NEW LOOK FOR YOU!' they heard a neighbour cry.

The door flew open again, hitting the wall with a bang. Mr Krampus was heaving with fury.

'You will regret the day you messed with me,' he hissed, throwing the hat at Rinki's feet before storming off.

And so Mr Krampus was gone. But he had no intention of leaving Blanche alone.

Chapter 10

Department Stores and Wrapping-Paper Hats

The 6th of December was for dancing through the snow at dusk, past jolly shoppers and candlelit windows. The streets smelt of crisp Christmas pine and cinnamon sticks. The butcher – an impossibly hairy man in a holly-covered apron – was lining up turkeys in the window.

'Hello, Miss Garland!' he called to Rinki. 'Tell Cook I'll save her the biggest turkey we've got!'

The milliner sang a Christmas tune and danced in the window she was decorating with white pom-poms made to look like falling snow. Across the street the florist handed out Christmas wreaths, while children in knitted mittens jumped for the mistletoe.

Carol singers flocked to a lamp post's glow, warming up their voices as they went. And on the corner the chocolatier emerged with a tray of tiny boxes wrapped in red ribbons.

'Miss Garland,' he said with a gentle bow, presenting the tray of chocolates. 'And Miss—'

'Claus,' Rinki said, opening a box and shoving the chocolate it contained in her mouth 'She's my best friend.'

Blanche let her own chocolate dissolve on her tongue and nodded her approval.

'We'll take nine each,' Rinki said.

'Why nine?' Blanche asked.

'It's my favourite number,' Rinki said, as she began handing the chocolates to the nearby children as soon as the chocolatier was out of sight.

On the 7th of December, they visited the department store, its painted toy soldiers standing proudly in the window beneath a canopy of crackers. Blanche reached into her pocket and wrapped her hand around her bauble.

'Come on,' Rinki said, dragging her inside the shop.

It wasn't long before Blanche began to feel uncomfortable. Her carter clothes and cap made her invisible on the streets, but in an establishment as grand as the department store it made her stand out more than the hairy butcher among his plucked turkeys.

'People are staring at me,' Blanche said.

'Well, let's give them something worth staring at,' said Rinki, taking the stairs two at a time to the first floor.

They bought a fancy hat for Teddy and a warm scarf for the captain and had them wrapped in ribbons and velvety paper. Rinki wore the hat around the shop – wrapped and on her head.

She linked arms with Blanche. 'Now they're staring at me and my ridiculous hat.'

On the 8th of December, Blanche hung her red bauble on the Garlands' Christmas tree.

'I'm happy it's there,' she said, and she felt happy there too.

On the 9th of December, Rinki and Blanche hid in a wardrobe and watched as the Queen had her fitting for the costume ball. She was draped in a black velvet dress with glittering chiffon sleeves.

'And what is that, my dear Teddy?' she asked, pointing at the red suit with the white trim.

'It's a design I've just finished, a little passion project,' he said.

'Quite stylish,' she said with approval.

'Thank you, ma'am,' Teddy replied. 'It feels special somehow, like it's waiting for a great adventure.'

'Aren't we all,' the Queen said with a sigh.

On the 10th of December, Blanche and Rinki watched Captain Garland pack for his next voyage. He would set sail in a few days for frosty lands, taking the iron box with him.

On the 11th of December, they threw snowballs at the strange men in suits, and braided Rudy's mane in clear sight of Mr Krampus. Rudy wasn't going anywhere.

On the 12th of December, they tried to open the box, using all the keys they could find in the house.

On the 13th of December, they decided there must be more keys that they would never find, so they built snowmen instead and draped them in Teddy's leftover fabrics. And then they spent the evening making paper snowflakes and dipping gingerbread in hot chocolate by firelight.

On the 14th of December, as Blanche was heading home, the servants of Stratton Street waited for her by the door with a basket full of steaming hot mince pies, tied with a ribbon and a sprig of mistletoe.

'Thought you'd be running low over at Christmas Lodge,' Cook said with a wink. 'See you tomorrow, dear girl.'

But tomorrow turned out to be very different to the days that had gone before it.

Chapter 11
The Secret

When Blanche returned to the docks that night, she was met by the three carter boys and they were acting suspiciously – flashing each other smug smiles and following her around but saying nothing.

'Would you like a mince pie?' she asked, holding up the basket and hoping it would make them go away. 'I have plenty.'

Whipper walked up and kicked it out of her hand. They all laughed as the delicious pies rolled towards the water, their perfect pastry coats covered in mud.

Blanche groaned inwardly. She should have seen that coming.

Sprout waved his fist in the air. 'We don't want your stinkin' mince pies! I bet they taste horrible.'

'We should've probably checked first,' Cole hissed, pulling one from the mud and giving it a sniff.

Blanche bowed her head and led Rudy across the yard to park the cart. As she filled a bucket with fistfuls of hay, she glanced back and saw the boys were edging closer. She felt her shoulders tense. It was never good when they showed an interest.

'We had a visitor today, Flimp,' Sprout blurted out, unable to keep the secret any longer.

Cole shoved him sideways.

'We were going to drag it out for longer!' he shouted. 'The plan was to wind him up with it!'

'Oh, why bother?' Whipper said, moving closer.

Blanche tried to block them out. She picked up a comb and began unpicking the knots in Rudy's mane.

'Guess who our visitor was. Go on!' Cole said as he and Sprout shoved Rudy out of the way.

Poor Rudy stumbled sideways and fell to her knees.

'STOP IT!' Blanche cried as she tried to help her up.

'Unusual visitor,' Whipper teased, grabbing Blanche's

arm. 'He had a strange cane – the type you don't forget in a hurry – and an even stranger story.'

Blanche froze. She felt her stomach fall to the ground, just as Rudy had done seconds before. She couldn't speak.

'I think Flimp knows who we're talking about,' Whipper said.

Blanche felt sick.

Mr Krampus.

'Look,' she began, hoping to reason with them. But she couldn't think what to say.

Whipper snatched her cap and her long white hair tumbled down.

'He *is* a girl! That Mr Krampus was right!' Sprout cheered.

Tears clouded her eyes, threatening to drop. 'She'll never work again!'

'We'll have the docks all to ourselves!'

'I can't believe Flimp's a girl!'

'What does it matter?' Blanche roared as tears spilt down her face, making the boys laugh even harder.

Blanche could see Rudy trying to get back on her feet.

'A GIRL!' the boys hooted.

'Yes, a girl,' Blanche snapped, the fury roaring through her like smoke through a chimney. 'A *girl* who's been better at carting than you *this whole time*.'

That made them stop laughing.

Rudy rose up behind the boys, but they were too busy to notice.

Cole looked giddy with glee. 'Well, you can say goodbye to that life now—'

Rudy whirled round and gave one almighty kick.

It was enough to take Cole clean off his feet. Blanche watched with some delight as he hit the ground, emerging after a moment's reflection with a full face of mud.

Sprout laughed so hard Cole leaped up and wrestled him to the ground.

Blanche took her chance and ran.

She tore across the yard, jumping over barrels and old anchors, and sleeping workers stirring to the cries of 'SHE'S GETTING AWAY!'.

She weaved between rickety sheds and broke through the hanging snow-soaked sacks sheltering tomorrow's shipments. She ducked down behind a barrel and saw the boys shoot off in different directions, flanking her so there was no route back to Rudy.

There was nowhere to go but the river.

She begrudgingly ducked down under the pier and slipped into the icy water. The shock of it made her gasp. She tried to think of a plan. She needed to get her and Rudy to Stratton Street. If she could get there, they'd be safe.

Her teeth clashed against each other and her whole body began to shudder. Her breath was coming in short, sharp bursts now. She couldn't stay in the water much longer.

She turned, desperately looking for another option, and saw the *Jolly Holly* floating in its berth, the river lapping gently at its grand bow.

She pulled herself up on to the pier, out of view of the boys, and ran to the ship.

'COME OUT, COME OUT WHEREVER YOU ARE!' Whipper teased menacingly, his voice echoing.

Blanche gritted her teeth and with her last nip of strength hauled herself aboard the *Jolly Holly*. The deck was slippery with snow and she skidded along it on her knees until she found a hatch. Inside, the bowels of the ship were empty and groaning with the rising tide. She wiped the dust off a porthole and the docks came into view. Rudy was where she'd left her, munching on her hay in the moonlight as if nothing out of the ordinary had occurred. The boys were running up and down, tipping over barrels and ripping open shed doors.

Blanche's eyes were growing heavy. The *Jolly Holly* felt safe. She grabbed a scratchy sack and climbed into it to try to warm up.

Only a few minutes had passed before the sound of boots on the deck above startled her awake.

'She's got to be here somewhere,' Whipper said loudly.

Blanche froze, afraid even to breathe.

'OI!' came an unfamiliar voice. 'THAT'S CAPTAIN GARLAND'S SHIP – STRICTLY CREW ONLY.'

The boys scarpered and Blanche collapsed in relief. She lay on her back, staring up at the ceiling, letting the movement of the ship gently rock her to sleep. She wriggled in the sack until it was up to her chin.

'Just a quick nap,' she said to herself. 'When the boys fall asleep, I'll grab Rudy and race to Rinki's house before they can stop me. An hour should be enough …'

Chapter 12
Trunks and Trouble

Blanche awoke to bright winter light streaming through the porthole. She yawned and tried to stretch her legs, but found she couldn't. When she sat up, she was met with a colossal pile of trunks towering in front of her – a wall of cargo that had not been there before.

Someone loading up the ship had clearly failed to notice the sleeping girl in the sack. She tried to get to the hatch, but the trunks were packed too tightly. She tried to move them, but they were immensely heavy – it was going to take hours.

The ship lurched and the sound of a hundred boots running on deck made the ceiling quake.

'Oh no,' Blanche said, her face turning as white as her hair. She peered out of the tiny porthole.

'NO!' she cried. The ship was moving out of the dock. 'No, no, no.' She tried desperately to move the trunks again.

'Rudy!'

Her hands were shaking and her eyes so filled with tears she could barely see what she was doing.

'RUDY!' she wailed.

The ship rocked from left to right and Blanche pressed her face miserably against the porthole. Rudy was on the dock, her neck bolt upright, her neighs frantic.

'RUDY!' Blanche cried. 'RUDY!'

The carter boys couldn't understand the commotion the horse was making. But when they saw the *Jolly Holly* setting sail, they put two and two together.

'YOU'VE GOT A GIRL HIDING ON YOUR SHIP!' they shouted, running alongside as the *Jolly Holly* headed downriver. 'YOU'VE GOT A GIRL HIDING ON YOUR SHIP!'

Blanche could hear the crew telling them to go away.

She stared out at Rudy, watching her get further and further away until finally she disappeared from view. Then she slumped in a heap among the trunks, her crying turning into desperate fits of sobbing.

She'd always told Rudy she would never leave her.

And now she might never see her again.

Chapter 13

Santa

'Helloooooo? Is there someone down here?' came a timid whisper. 'I really hope you're not a ghost.'

It had been a day and a night since the ship had left London, but Blanche hadn't stopped crying. It was the thought of Rudy alone and scared on the docks, and Rinki wondering why she hadn't met her as planned. The torture of not knowing how long she'd be at sea and if she would ever find her way home. The irony of having been trapped by the very things she was employed to move.

So hearing a voice – though startling at first – filled her with relief.

She wiped away her tears and shuffled closer to the trunks to get a better look.

Through the gaps, she could just make out the light of a candle moving shakily back and forth.

'Is there anybody there?' came the voice again.

Quickly, she moved back and curled up against the wall. She wondered if she could trust him, or would he brand her a stowaway and throw her overboard?

'My name's Santa,' the voice said. 'I thought I heard crying. If you are a ghost, or anything like that, I just want you to know that I come down here to cry too. So we probably have a lot in common. Therefore, I conclude there is no need to haunt, eat or otherwise torture me. Um, please?'

He sounded sweet, Blanche decided.

Next came a rattle of tin on the floor, as if someone were hastily laying the table for dinner. The smell of sweet mince pies made her scuttle forward. Earlier in the day, and with a lot of effort, she had managed to rearrange the trunks. One more push and she could squeeze over to his side.

'Remember you're *brave*. Remember you're *brave*.

Yes, they're polar explorers and you just cook their food, but you're brave too,' the voice said.

Carefully, Blanche moved closer to get a better look. She inched the trunks apart and candlelight flooded through the gap. She could just make out a boy around her age wearing a cook's hat and sitting cross-legged on the floor.

'Yes, you're afraid of being at sea and no it's not brave to hide down here and have midnight feasts to make yourself feel better. But you are, by association, a *brave* explorer too, Santa. Yes. You. Are.'

The boy had brought a little feast of mince pies with him and a mug of hot chocolate, which he'd placed neatly in front of him.

He had big kind eyes and eyebrows so bushy that if you tipped him upside down they would have looked like a beard.

The thought made Blanche snort, which he must have heard, because –

'Hello?' he said suddenly.

Blanche jumped, sending the very highest trunk toppling to the floor. It crashed open and a torrent of

Christmas baubles tumbled out and shattered at the boy's feet.

He leaped up, brandishing a mince pie.

'I'm armed!' he shouted, which made Blanche burst out laughing.

She squeezed her way through the trunk wall and waved.

'That's a mince pie.'

'I know.' Santa sighed. 'What are you doing down here? You're not crew – you don't have a green waistcoat.'

'I'm Blanche Claus, and I shouldn't be here. But unfortunately, I am.'

'And, er, did you hear those things I was saying to myself?'

His cheeks were turning crimson.

'I heard a little bit,' Blanche said.

His face crumpled. 'Oh.'

'But for what it's worth, I think everyone on this ship is a brave explorer.'

'I'm technically just the cook,' he said. 'So what are you doing on the *Jolly Holly*?'

'Crying, mostly,' Blanche said with a sad smile. 'I got stuck down here and the ship set sail. I left my … my …' The thought of Rudy neighing frantically on the docks was too much, and Blanche burst into tears again.

'Oh no, don't cry,' Santa said. 'You'll set me off.'

He held out a mince pie for Blanche and then he burst into tears as well.

'I find mince pies make me feel better,' he sobbed.

'My best friend loves mince pies!' Blanche howled, the thought of Rinki making her cry even harder.

To stop herself, she shoved the entire mince pie in her mouth in one go, Rinki style. It was buttery and comforting.

'I think that was the best mince pie I've ever eaten,' she sniffed when she was able to speak again.

'I made them,' Santa said. His face brightened a little. 'Have as many as you like. Captain Garland said he wanted a cook who could make mince pies like his cook's at Stratton Street. He said mine might be even better! His cook said if she ever saw me again, she'd make *me* into a mince pie. I'm still not sure if she meant it.'

Blanche thought Cook probably *was* fierce enough to bake Santa into a mince pie but decided not to mention it.

'I'd say you're safe at sea,' she said instead.

Santa handed Blanche his hot chocolate and they settled down on the floor.

'What are you going to do now?'

Blanche shrugged sadly. 'I don't think there's anything I can do. I'm stuck on a ship.'

'We should tell Captain Garland,' Santa said. 'He might be able to turn the ship around! I'd quite like that, to be honest.'

'I can't tell him!' Blanche cried. 'Captain Garland is my best friend's father – I'll be in so much trouble. He'll think I'm dreadful for sneaking on to the ship. What if he never lets me see Rinki again?'

Santa sat in silence for a moment. 'Well, let me help you at least,' he said with a smile. 'I can bring you meals and treats to make you feel better until we think of a way to get you out of this mess.'

Blanche felt a surge of relief.

'Actually, I was wondering how I would get food.'

'I know,' Santa said. 'Not much nutritional value in a Christmas bauble.'

'MY BAUBLE!' Blanche cried, making Santa leap to his feet.

She dug her hand deep into her pocket. Her heart sank when her fingers hit the bottom.

'I left it on Rinki's tree.'

'Um,' Santa said, his face a mixture of confusion and mild alarm. 'If it's a bauble you're after, you did spill quite a few of them on the floor earlier.'

He gestured all around them.

'The one thing you do have right now – in abundance – is baubles.'

'It wasn't an ordinary bauble,' Blanche muttered.

'Well,' Santa said slowly, clearly struggling to find the right words but keen to do his best. 'Everything is going to be all right, Blanche Claus. I'll be back in the morning with breakfast.'

'You're a saint, Santa,' Blanche said. 'And a wonderful friend already.'

Santa was true to his word. Every morning and evening he arrived with a long sock stuffed with food. Each meal was more delicious than the last, and over the next week she and Santa became firm friends.

They were both orphans.

'Yet another orphan!' Blanche said, throwing her hands in the air. 'What are the chances?'

They talked with relish about Yule logs and mince pies as they dipped Christmas cookies in hot chocolate. Blanche salvaged some of the baubles and decorated her hiding place until it looked like a twinkly Christmas grotto in the candlelight. Santa sewed a B on to Blanche's sock and gave her the orange he'd won in a card game against Captain Garland. Each night they ate and laughed until it was way past midnight and their stomachs and hearts were full.

It was during one of their midnight feasts that the accident happened.

The storm had been building for hours, and as Blanche and Santa sang Christmas songs by candlelight,

they heard the first crack of thunder above the ship.

'What was that?' Santa said, shuffling closer to Blanche.

'Oh, it's just the storm,' Blanche said breezily, launching into song again.

A moment later, the ship rocked violently and struck something with such force that Blanche and Santa were catapulted across the hold. The candle went out and they sat in the darkness.

'That sounded like more than a storm,' Santa squeaked.

Footsteps thundered overhead. There was another crack and the planks above them began to split, dripping light from the deck into the luggage hold.

'This is bad,' Santa whispered, his voice shaking. 'I – I suppose I'd better go and see what's happened.'

He hesitated as he got to his feet and smiled meekly.

'I'll be back soon,' he promised, before climbing up through the hatch.

The floor around Blanche was littered with smashed baubles and mangled mince pies. She picked one up and blew the dust from it, feeling almost sorry for it. Rinki's deep respect for mince pies was obviously rubbing off on her.

Above her, the ship's crew were racing back and forth, jumping over the hatch Santa had left open.

'Blasted iceberg,' she heard Captain Garland say. 'Get me the coordinates of the last ship we passed.'

He tripped over the hatch.

'AND KEEP THIS BLASTED THING CLOSED!' he ordered.

Something fell from his pocket. Something shiny.

Blanche held out her hand to catch it and it landed perfectly in her palm, just as the hatch closed with a bang.

Her pulse quickened. It was cold. Metal. She traced the lines of it with her fingers – snowflakes.

It was the keys to the mysterious box.

She turned in the near darkness, wondering if it might be down there.

Her toe hit iron instantly, and she couldn't tell if she had found the box or the box had found her.

She fumbled with the complicated locks.

Finally, she would get to see what was inside!

The last key clicked into place and she turned it slowly, causing the lid to pop open, just a sliver.

Blanche was about to open it fully, but a tiny hand got there first.

She backed away quickly, but not quickly enough – the thing shot out and grabbed on to her eyelids.

'YOU SAVED ME!' it cheered, its eyes wild, taking in the surroundings and Blanche in one excitable gulp.

'I'M CAROL!' it said. Then it sniffed the air. 'We're close to home!'

It was no bigger than Blanche's thumb and looked like a fairy, with glittering candy-cane striped hair and bright green eyes.

'Carol?' Blanche managed, feeling completely bewildered.

The fairy jumped up and down on her bottom lip.

'That's right – Carol. Those beasts up there have been keeping me hostage for months and months. They caught me when I was floating on a sheet of ice in no man's land. I wasn't even lost – it was a very specific piece of ice. Punishment ice, actually. The other Carols made me go there. I bet they're worried. But then again, I bet they're not. Well, maybe they might be—'

'Other Carols?' Blanche said. 'There are more of you?'

'Thousands,' Carol said.

'And you're all called Carol?'

Carol nodded. 'It's a good name.'

'Why were you on a piece of punishment ice?' Blanche asked, feeling slightly worried the tiny thing might be some sort of dangerous mini criminal.

Carol flew down and kicked the box into the corner with such force Blanche thought it might shoot through the side of the ship. Clearly she was dealing with a very powerful creature indeed.

'I was being punished,' Carol said.

'Why?' Blanche asked, as she heard a crash overhead.

Carol looked away, her little wings drooping. 'I was bad. I went rogue.'

'You ... committed a crime?'

The fairy nodded. 'A HORRIBLE CRIME! I used magic to make a friend.'

'That doesn't sound very criminal to me,' Blanche said, and she felt her shoulders untense.

'But the friend isn't like me, he's ... It's a long story. The short of it is, I got captured by Captain Garland and his crew. Why are they making all that noise, anyway?'

'We've hit an iceberg,' Blanche said. 'It sounds bad.'

'Really?' the fairy said, sounding far too excited. 'Well, Blanche Claus, I think this is my moment!'

'How do you know my name?' Blanche asked in amazement.

'I was in the box,' the fairy said flatly. 'You introduced yourself to Santa while you were very close to the box. And Rinki shouted your name when you delivered me to Stratton Street. I have ears, you know.'

Blanche laughed nervously at the thought that the fairy had listened to a whole day and night of her wailing.

The fairy flew up to her shoulder and patted her on the head. 'Don't worry about the crying. I've been back and forth on this ship a few times now and it's usually that Santa one that's crying. I like your cry better, it's less ... what's the word ... *snotty*.'

'Thanks, I think,' Blanche said.

'Now, if you'll excuse me, I need to GET MY REVENGE AND SINK THIS SHIP!'

'Wait, no, don't—'

But the fairy cut her off. 'IT'S THE ONLY THING FOR IT!'

'It's not!' Blanche spluttered, thinking of Santa and Captain Garland and all the other people on board. But Carol flipped the hatch open and flew off into the night.

'Carol! There are other options!'

Carol popped her head back into the hold.

'It's sinking anyway, and this way I can use the Box Revenge Plan that I've been plotting for months!'

'Carol, I really don't think that's a good idea,' Blanche warned, but the little creature had vanished.

Blanche swallowed a whimper. 'What have I done?' she whispered, staring at the box lying open on the floor.

There was a flash of candy-cane light and the ship lurched.

A loud hissing drowned out the sound of the shouting men above, and Blanche watched in horror as water burst through the side of the hold.

'Blanche!' she heard Santa cry above her. An arm reached down, but as Blanche made a grab for it, the ship lurched again, sending Santa hurtling out of sight.

'SANTA!' she shouted frantically. 'SANTA!'

The water began to creep fast, up past her waist, then her shoulders, until she could taste the salt in her mouth.

She dragged herself across the trunks, trying to get higher, but the ship lurched a final time, and everything went black.

Blanche floated unconscious in her sunken hiding place, surrounded by broken baubles and the sock with a B sewn on it.

But it wasn't the end of her story. Later she would look back and see it as a beginning.

Chapter 14

The Disaster

Blanche hadn't visited in over a week and Rinki knew something was wrong. Teddy had promised to take her down to the docks, but things kept coming up – the latest, a last-minute showcase of his new dress designs at the department store. With the Garlands' carriage gone, and Rinki growing increasingly worried, she decided there was only one thing for it – she would walk to the docks, and she would go alone.

'You're a bit posh for round here!' a man shouted as she passed. She'd been hoping to go unnoticed and had

worn her most subtle cape – purple velvet with sequin angel wings on the back.

It was as subtle as Rinki's wardrobe got.

The docks smelt foul and the mud beneath her boots made it feel like she was wading through figgy pudding. The spot where Captain Garland's ship had been docked was being used by a small passenger vessel with a holey canopy. No one appeared to be waiting to sail in it.

'Fancy a boat trip, miss?' said the man loitering nearby. 'You look like you could hire this whole glorious boat for yourself. It's got comfy seats and great views.' He shoved a hand through one of the holes in the canopy. 'You can see straight to the sky!'

'That does sound wonderful,' Rinki said. 'But I'm looking for a friend.'

'Well, you're looking in the wrong place! I doubt your friend would come down here. You want to look back in proper London, on them nice streets with the pretty lights and carol singers.'

'No, I'm in the right place,' Rinki said. She pressed a mince pie into the man's hand. 'I'd be grateful if you could show me where to find the carters though.'

The man looked at the mince pie and licked his lips. 'Certainly, miss. Just inside that stone hut is where they'll be. And you'll see their horses just round the corner. Look, there's one of 'em now.'

Rinki's heart sank when Rudy appeared with another carter riding her. It was hardly riding, really. More just kicking.

'STOP THAT!' Rinki cried, staggering through the mud.

'Stupid horse, go fast like you do for Flimp!'

Rinki wobbled. The mud was thick and practically up to her shins. 'Where – where's the carter who rides that horse?' she demanded, trying to hide her fear. Blanche had told her stories about the carter boys, and she knew the sooner she got out of there the better.

Whipper laughed as the others emerged from the hut and surrounded her.

Rinki gulped.

'Who wants to know?' Cole asked, while Sprout pulled on Rudy's mane for the fun of it.

'It's not important who I am,' Rinki said, standing tall. 'Where's "Flimp"?'

112

'We're not tellin' you anything,' Whipper said.

'He got on Captain Garland's boat. But he's a *girl*! A man called Mr Krampus told us!' Sprout blurted out, unable to keep the secret any longer.

Whipper rounded on him. 'You really have a problem with keeping secrets, don't you?'

Rinki was reeling. Mr Krampus had told them she was a girl. Blanche was on the *Jolly Holly*?

'When we – ah, er – confronted her about it, she ran away and sailed off on the ship,' Cole said, dismounting Rudy and landing with a squelch in the mud. 'So now the horse is ours. Just need to figure out how she made it go so fast.'

Rinki looked downriver and towards the sea, smiling at the thought of Blanche sailing across the world. She couldn't decide whether she was furious with Mr Krampus or delighted that he'd accidentally given Blanche a new adventure.

Rudy exhaled loudly. Clearly she was peeved about being left alone with the boys.

'I'll take the horse,' Rinki said.

'No, you won't!' Whipper shouted. 'We're still usin' it!'

Rudy stared at Rinki, and she was sure she saw the horse wink. Then she lifted a hoof and seemed to point at the river.

'And you can't keep starin' at it,' Whipper snapped. 'It's *our* horse, now go away!'

Rinki nodded and began wading through the mud towards the river, constantly looking back at the horse, who seemed to be nodding and willing her on.

'Town's that way!' Cole laughed. 'You going to swim home or something?'

Rinki's boots hit the pier just as Sprout screamed, 'LOOK!'

Rudy bucked and jumped, her back legs flying in all directions, whipping up a storm of mud.

Rinki watched in amazement as Rudy then shot towards her. Before she had a moment to think, the horse scooped her up with her nose and leaped off the pier into the river.

'IT'S GETTING AWAY!' Cole screeched. 'IT'S SWIMMING!'

Rinki choked on river water as she heaved herself on to Rudy's back. Then, like an elegant swan, they took off downstream as if it were the most normal thing in the world.

The man with the holey boat was licking the last of the mince pie off his fingers when he saw something that made his eyes grow wide.

'Get what you came here for?' he called, as Rinki and Rudy sailed down the river.

'Almost!' Rinki said, glancing back at the three carter boys covered in mud.

The man tipped his cap at her.

'If you see the other carter, the one they call Flimp,' Rinki shouted to him, 'be sure to pass on the message that Rudy is safe at Stratton Street!'

Rinki arrived home soaked, stinking and feeling triumphant. She took Rudy to the stables and gave her a bucket of carrots.

Teddy stood in the doorway, his face white and his eyes distant.

'Before you say anything, let me explain,' Rinki said quickly, sensing she was in trouble. 'I really needed to go

to the docks. And it's good that I did, because I saved Rudy. Blanche boarded the *Jolly Holly* and has sailed off on an adventure! I'm not sure she meant to, but at least she's safe.'

Teddy held on to the door frame to steady himself. 'Blanche … Blanche was on board the *Jolly Holly*?'

Rinki laughed. 'Don't look so shocked! She deserves an adventure!'

'Rinki, I have something …' Teddy began, but the words fizzled out as soon as they hit the frosty air.

Rudy looked up, her nostrils flared and her eyes wide.

'What is it?' Rinki asked, looking from Teddy to the horse and back again.

'Rinki, the *Jolly Holly* sank, I just got word of it.'

Rinki stumbled backwards and crumpled in a heap on the snowy step.

'And where are the people on board?'

Teddy shook his head sadly. 'No one has been found.'

Chapter 15
Crackling Candy Canes

When Blanche came to, she was being dragged through the snow by a squat little elf creature with an iron-tight grip on her ankles.

It took her a moment to realise that it was not a normal scenario, and she should probably fear for her life.

'WHO ARE YOU?!' she screamed, trying to break free.

The elf creature stopped. 'I'm *Carol*,' she said, sounding more than a tad miffed. 'We met on the ship? You've been out for a few days, so you've forgotten me!'

'YOU'RE NOT CAROL – CAROL WAS A BEAUTIFUL FAIRY!'

The elf was nothing like Carol. She had long ears like a rabbit but stuck to the sides of her head. Like Carol, she had candy-cane striped hair, but that was where the similarity ended. There was just a tiny tuft of it on her head, and some in her ears.

'WHAT HAVE YOU DONE TO CAROL THE FAIRY?' Blanche demanded.

The elf waddled up to her face and leaned over until they were nose to nose. 'I *am* Carol. Fairies and elves are the *same thing*. We just look different in different temperatures. Once it gets below minus-twenty degrees, we look a little bit more like this. What do you think ELF stands for?'

'Um,' Blanche mumbled. 'I didn't know it stood for anything. I thought it just meant elf?'

Carol rolled her eyes. 'Elf – E.L.F. – stands for Einfrieren Little Fairy.'

'What does Einfrieren mean?' Blanche asked.

'It's German for freezing. ELF means Freezing Little Fairy. Now, can I please continue pulling you by the ankles?'

Blanche sprang to her feet. 'No, no, it's fine. I'm happy to walk.'

'Suit yourself,' Carol said, marching on ahead.

Blanche took one step and fell face first into the snow. She raised an arm. 'Actually, I could do with a little help please, Carol.'

Carol grabbed her ankles and carried on pulling. 'I found this on the ship before it went under.' She stopped pulling for a moment and held up the sock with the B on it. 'I thought you might want it.'

'SANTA!' Blanche cried, staring at the sock.

'Gesundheit,' Carol said.

'I wasn't sneezing!' Blanche said. 'Santa was a cook on the ship, remember? Big eyebrows, cries a bit. Is he safe? Did you save him too?'

'He's almost certainly in the box,' Carol said.

'A coffin?' Blanche wailed. 'He's *dead*?'

'*The box*,' Carol said. 'I put all the crew in it and sent them sailing home! It's got iron stars on it and everything, just like the one they locked me in, only bigger. I thought it would be poetic.'

'So they're alive?'

Carol stopped dead in her tracks and turned, her eyes straining with surprise. 'I'm *an elf*, Blanche, not a murderer. They are all safe in a floating box and will arrive back where they came from very soon. And the *Jolly Holly* will reappear in a few days, as good as new.'

Blanche stared at her with her mouth hanging open. Carol, who was clearly enjoying the easily wowed audience, puffed up her chest and continued.

'I think they were trying to investigate the lands around here – snoop a little. Well, "explorers", FEEL MY TINY WRATH AND ENJOY YOUR TRIP ALL THE WAY BACK HOME!'

She smiled a satisfied smile and forged on ahead.

'You … you can do all that?' Blanche asked in awe.

Carol turned and stared at her again.

'Oh yes, of course, sorry – you're an *elf*.'

'We have so much magic,' Carol said with a sigh, 'and nothing to do with it. Elves are very strict, and using my magic is what gets me in trouble. So, so much *trouble*.'

Blanche let Carol drag her along in silence for a while. There was nothing but snow and pretty fir trees all around them, and even though she should have been freezing, aside from the frost moustache, she was perfectly warm. It was as if heat radiated from Carol's tiny hands, warming every inch of her.

'Where are we going?' Blanche asked.

'Home,' Carol said.

'London?' Blanche asked hopefully.

'No.' Carol stopped and pulled Blanche to her feet. 'It's a little different to London. I thought you might like it as a present for saving me. I'm taking you somewhere *no* human has been before.'

Blanche watched in amazement as a candy cane rose up from the snow in front of them.

There was a crackle. It sounded to Blanche like kindling on a fire.

'What is it?' she said, but Carol quickly held a finger to her lips.

A voice boomed from the candy cane. 'Please identify yourself! The Carols currently out of bounds are: Carol floating on the punishment ice for breaking the elf code – now AWOL. Then there's Carol who keeps sneaking off to the Polar Tavern to drink bear-sized bottles of mulled wine, and Carol and Carol, the twins, who have not been seen in a long time.'

'The first one,' Carol said with a resigned sigh.

Another crackle. 'Really?'

'Yes, I made it home after a long and terrifying ordeal with some humans.'

There was a chorus of gasps and Blanche realised others were listening too.

'Ah! It's a strange and magical communication device thing!' Blanche said, giving it a tap. 'I thought it was the candy cane itself speaking.'

'Who was that?' The voice sounded alarmed.

Carol laughed nervously and chewed at a fingernail. 'It was – well … it was … actually *me.*'

'No it wasn't. That voice was big. You haven't got a human with you, have you?'

Carol gulped. 'No.'

'Are you sure you don't? Because that would be … unprecedented.'

Blanche stared anxiously at Carol and waited for her to admit it, and maybe ask – or beg – if she could come in. But all Carol said was –

'Mmess.'

She covered the end of the candy cane with her hand, a cheeky glint in her eye. 'If I don't say yes then it's not a lie.'

'Was that a yes?'

She leaned closer and gave Blanche a wink. 'Mmess!'

Blanche was beginning to wonder if there was a point at which she should have stopped the elf with a criminal record dragging her through the snow to bypass some sort of edible security system.

'I'm sorry, the line is a little crackly, could you—?'

'MMESS!'

'APPROVED. Welcome home, Carol!'

The candy cane began to glow, and Carol's hair glowed too.

In an instant, a flurry of snow whipped around them and the trees seemed to bend and blur, as if the whole world were a spinning top.

'Carol!' Blanche cried as her feet lifted off the ground. She felt around for something to grab hold of, but there was only snow. 'CAROL?!'

'Mmess?' Carol called back with an amused snort,

and then everything slowed. The blizzard eased and a magical sight met Blanche's eyes.

Where just a few moments earlier there had been only white, there was now a sprawling town of elf-sized buildings made with gingerbread-men bricks and snow. Technicolor icicles hung from the trees and candy-cane lamp posts lined the streets.

'Welcome to Carolburg!' Carol said.

Blanche's eyes had grown as big as puddings. 'It's – it's …'

She knew this place.

'You're the first human to see it,' Carol said. 'Expect a strong reaction from the other Carols.'

Chapter 16

Same, Same, Same, Same, Same, Same ...

'LISTEN UP, EVERYONE. CAROL IS BACK ... AND SHE'S BROUGHT A HUMAN!'

The hysteria was deafening. All across town, elves screeched and screamed and ran in circles, occasionally knocking themselves out on candy-cane lamp posts.

Blanche held her hands to her ears to block out the noise as tiny gingerbread-men-shaped doors slammed and wrapping-paper curtains were hastily drawn.

'They'll calm down,' Carol said, sounding a little unsure. 'They will ...'

Blanche followed her through the now eerily silent

town, stepping over low strings of icicles as she went. They passed a long communal dining table made of glistening ice and a beautiful skating rink soaked in technicolor light, before arriving at the workshop.

'It's the only place big enough for you,' Carol said, pushing open the creaky gingerbread doors.

Blanche ducked inside, being careful not to hit her head on the ceiling – something told her gingerbread was not the most durable of building materials.

It was cute, and even though it was empty, there was something homely about it. Or maybe it was the strange and familiar town itself that made Blanche feel instantly at home.

'We used this as a place to design and make parts for the other buildings in town, but we finished years and years ago, so the workshop lies empty.'

'Couldn't you just use magic to build everything?' Blanche asked.

'We could,' Carol said. 'But we have nothing to do and we're really bored. At least building things takes a while. Especially with gingerbread, because SOMEONE –' she mouthed *me* – 'always eats it!'

'You're bored?'

'So bored,' Carol said, plopping down on an old stack of gingerbread-men-shaped bricks and taking a bite. 'The elf code is very strict, and we have nothing to do except be elves.'

'What's the elf code?' Blanche asked.

'All elves must act the same, and dress the same, and do the same things, and eat the same things, mostly at the same time. If you step out of line, you get banished to the floating sheet of punishment ice, like I was. Carolburg is not as magical as you'd imagine it to be.'

Blanche gazed out of the window. 'It's pretty magical to me, just like the first time I saw it, all those years ago.'

'*I beg your pardon?*' Carol said, practically choking on some gingerbread.

Blanche told her about the mysterious old woman, and the bauble and the magical little world inside it that was *definitely* Carolburg.

Carol nodded knowingly. 'You can always count on an old woman to really get things going. Let's see the bauble, then.'

Blanche reached into her pocket for it. Her face fell.

'I keep forgetting I don't have it – I left it on Rinki's tree.'

'Convenient,' Carol said.

'I'm not making it up! Didn't you hear Rinki and me talking about it in the study at Stratton Street?'

Carol shrugged. 'Don't think so.'

'But you said earlier that's how you knew my name – that you had ears and—'

'I also have a routine,' Carol said. 'Including *sleep*. Maybe I was out for the count. Or maybe you're making it all up. It doesn't sound very believable.'

'You're an *elf*. A *magic elf*,' Blanche scoffed. She could feel herself getting frustrated with the tiny creature. 'I'm not making it up.'

They stood in moody silence for a second, then Blanche remembered something.

'I saw a thing in the bauble that isn't here.' She paused. 'This is going to sound completely mad, but I also saw … a giant dancing Christmas tree.'

Carol suddenly looked panicked. It was not the reaction Blanche expected.

'Keep your voice down,' Carol begged. 'He'll hear—'

The snow beneath their feet began to quake.

'What was that?' Blanche asked nervously, fearing it might be the sound of a coordinated attack. Death by a thousand Carols was not the way she wanted to go.

Carol ran to the window and looked up to the icy mountains surrounding the town. 'There's only one thing that causes that rumble.'

'EGGGGGNOGGGGG!' came a bellow that nearly knocked them over.

Blanche raced outside to see a giant fir tree with long leafy eyelashes and a huge grin bounding towards them.

'It's real!' Blanche squealed with delight.

'Oh yes. That's what I did with my magic,' Carol said, hanging her head in shame as the enchanted tree crashed through the town.

She waved reluctantly, forcing a smile. 'He's called Eggnog.'

'He's wonderful!' Blanche cried.

The tree ground to a screeching halt.

'Uh-oh,' Carol said.

'CAROL IS BACK!' the tree bellowed when he

spotted her. He scrunched up his face at Blanche. 'AND A JUMBO ELF!'

He hopscotched towards them, flattening houses as he went.

'He's too big for the town,' Carol said as a couple of elves emerged from the rubble and glared at her.

Eggnog lunged at Blanche, engulfing her in a leafy hug. She wriggled around to dodge the twigs.

'Eggnog meet Blanche Claus, Blanche Claus meet Eggnog,' Carol said with all the enthusiasm of a melted snowman. 'She saved me from some human captors.'

'YOU SAVED MY MUMMY!?' Eggnog cried as snow tears filled his eyes.

'No,' Carol said. 'We've gone over this, Eggnog. I'm an *elf*, I used magic to make you real but I'm not your mummy. You came from seeds from other trees. *Trees*, Eggnog.'

But Eggnog wasn't listening. 'BLANCHE IS A HERO!' he roared, hugging her tighter.

'Ow,' Blanche squeaked. 'My bones.'

'WELCOME TO THE NORTH POLE, BLANCHE!'

Blanche hugged the tree back, carefully at first, but

soon she was melting happily into him. There was something comforting about an Eggnog hug. It was like being wrapped in Christmas.

'He does give very good hugs, once you learn how to avoid the twigs,' Carol said from where she was perched, high above Blanche's head. Eggnog was covered in decorations that jingled cheerily as Carol climbed higher. Blanche could just make out the little elf through the thick foliage as she clawed her way to the top and grabbed hold of the very tip of the tree.

'But the problem is,' Carol shouted down, 'he never likes to LET GO!'

'What?' Blanche shouted.

'LET GO OF BLANCHE, EGGNOG!' Carol ordered, shaking him. 'LET GO!'

'HUGS FOREVER!'

'No,' Carol said firmly. 'Hugs for an appropriate length of time, as discussed.'

Eggnog reluctantly let Blanche go.

'It's important to think magic through,' Carol said, 'or else you could end up with a tree that—'

'HUGS FOREVER!' Eggnog cheered.

'And *that*,' said another Carol at Blanche's feet, 'is why we don't go rogue with magic. Some call it creativity, I call it DANGER.'

'He flattens our town!' another cried. 'He squashes the lot!'

'He's too big and too clumsy!' another screeched.

Blanche stared at the enchanted Christmas tree in amazement. 'I think he's the most marvellous thing I've ever seen.'

'Well, of course you *would* think that,' another Carol scoffed. 'You're not an elf.'

'I wish I was,' Blanche said, as more and more of them gathered around her. She thought the ability to sink ships and create enchanted Christmas trees might be worth becoming an elf for.

Carol rearranged some of Eggnog's Christmas ornaments, like a mother buttoning up a child's school shirt. 'Now, off you go, Eggnog, back to the mountains. You can't stay here.'

Eggnog smiled sadly at Blanche. 'I'M SORRY, BLANCHE. I HAVE TO GO.' And off he went.

'Surely he could live in Carolburg?' Blanche said.

All the Carols shook their heads.

Blanche watched Eggnog make short work of several gingerbread houses in the few strides it took for him to clear the town.

'I wish he *could* stay,' Carol whispered to Blanche. 'I tried to make him float so he wouldn't crush our homes. I've tried everything.'

'The floating didn't work?' Blanche asked.

Carol shook her head. 'It made him feel sick, and I was banished to the punishment ice before I could try anything else. I think it's better for him in the mountains, the elves are too scared to be nice to him.'

She paused and looked up at Blanche with a glint in her eye.

'Speaking of floating, there's something I've been meaning to do!' And off she ran, her hair glowing suspiciously.

Chapter 17
Rinki Knows It's Magic

The snow was falling thick and fast when the large floating box stamped with iron stars arrived in London, docking like a ship in the very spot Captain Garland's *Jolly Holly* had left from.

The top flipped open and the crew scrambled out in terror, tearing off into the city before Captain Garland – who was the last to emerge – could bid them goodnight.

At the stroke of midnight he walked through the door of 6 Stratton Street. His arrival was cause for much celebration, and Teddy and Cook's joyful shrieks were enough to wake Rinki from her sleep. She quickly pulled on her dressing gown and flung herself on to the banister, sliding down the three floors before landing with an enormous thud in the entrance hall.

Despite the noise she'd made, Captain Garland and Teddy were too busy talking to notice her.

'It *sank* the ship?' Teddy said with a gasp.

'I am certain of it,' Captain Garland replied. 'The tiny creature escaped from the box and set about sinking us! We'd struck an iceberg and were sinking anyway, but the little thing finished us off!'

'Are you sure you didn't imagine it?' Teddy reasoned.

'You saw it yourself, Ted. We both know that creature is real. And look, it left me the little empty box.'

Rinki inched nearer, eager to hear more.

'I wish I'd been the one to set it free,' Captain Garland said, clenching his fists in frustration. 'I was so close to returning it to where we found it.'

'It sounds like it was perfectly capable of finding its own way home,' Teddy said. 'Keeping it in the box was the worst thing you could have done.'

'It proves my theory that there must be a magical world out there somewhere,' Captain Garland said. 'It seems like it's more magical than anything we've ever imagined.'

'All I know is that if that thing hadn't put you in a box and sailed you back here, you would have died at sea.'

Captain Garland chuckled. 'I think the box was the creature's way of teaching us a lesson.'

Rinki couldn't help herself any longer. 'Are you talking about what was in the box?'

'Rinki!' Captain Garland said, scooping her up in a big hug.

'Is Blanche all right?' she asked desperately, her words tumbling into each other in her eagerness for an answer. 'Where is she? Did you find her?'

'Blanche?' Captain Garland asked.

'You know, ice-white hair – my best friend Blanche!' she said.

'But Blanche wasn't on my ship, Rinki.' His face looked pained. 'We lost only one person, a young boy, a cook called Santa.'

Rinki's eyes welled with tears.

'Is Blanche missing?' Captain Garland asked.

136

'She boarded your ship! She can't be gone! You must be mistaken!'

There was a clatter from the stables.

'That must be her!' Rinki wiped the tears fiercely from her eyes and raced down the hall.

When she flung open the back door, a grim voice greeted her in the darkness.

'Oh, I thought you'd be asleep by now.'

Rinki whimpered. There, standing in flickering candlelight, was Mr Krampus.

A smile snaked across his face. 'I did warn you.'

Then a gruff-looking man, lacking in height and hair and wearing a blood-splattered apron, emerged from the shadows. Rinki could just make out his battered cart drawn up next to the stables. It was large and empty, as though it were waiting for something.

She watched in horror as Mr Krampus unhooked the door to Rudy's stable.

'I thought you had listened to me,' he said. 'The horse went away for a few glorious days, and now it's back.'

'Yes, but in a *stable*,' Rinki pointed out. 'You didn't like it on the street.'

Mr Krampus shrugged. 'I don't want it anywhere. She's old and useless anyway – but not useless to the glue factory.'

Rinki scrambled across the courtyard and tried to prise Mr Krampus's fingers from Rudy's halter.

'STOP IT! SHE'S STAYING HERE!'

Mr Krampus gave the man in the bloodstained apron a nod. He shoved Rinki out of the way and grabbed Rudy by the halter, pulling her towards the cart.

'Now just wait a second!' Teddy shouted as he appeared in the doorway, his eyes wide and wild.

Rinki bit the glue man's hand, but it was no good – he had a firm grip on Rudy and he wasn't letting go.

'Give the horse to the glue man, there's a good girl,' Mr Krampus said.

'NO!' Rinki cried. 'Teddy, do something!'

'Mr Krampus,' Teddy said sternly. 'Stop this madness!'

Captain Garland stepped outside. 'It's not your horse, Krampus!' he bellowed. 'You have no right to take it away.'

But there was no reasoning with Mr Krampus, he was enjoying it too much.

Rinki grabbed hold of Rudy's mane and clung on as tightly as she could.

'If she doesn't let go,' Mr Krampus said, practically squealing with delight, 'then the girl will go for glue too!'

Captain Garland set upon him and clamped his hand firmly on the man's shoulder. 'Choose your words wisely, Krampus.'

Poor Rudy was terrified as she was dragged towards the cart. She and Rinki frantically tried to dig their heels in as they bounced along the cobbles.

It was then that the most peculiar thing happened.

Rudy's mane flashed in candy-cane coloured stripes.

The glue man jumped back in fright.

'WHAT ON EARTH IS THE MATTER WITH YOU?' Mr Krampus snapped. 'TAKE THE HORSE FROM HER!'

Everyone else fell silent and stared at the mane.

Even Rudy stood strangely still, as if she too were surprised.

Her mane flashed again – the same candy-coloured stripes.

'DID YOU SEE THAT?!' Mr Krampus shrieked,

wriggling out of Captain Garland's grip and pulling hard on the horse's mane.

Rudy's hooves scraped and slipped in the snow as she tried to get away from him.

'Stop it! You're hurting her!' Rinki cried.

'HER MANE CHANGED COLOUR!' Mr Krampus roared.

There was another flash and this time Rudy's hooves became candy-cane striped. They glowed brighter and brighter until the horse took off from the ground, rising up and up until she was out of reach. Rinki stumbled backwards and watched in amazement.

'WHO IS DOING THAT?' Mr Krampus screamed. 'TELL ME WHO!'

He stared down at Rinki, his face a mixture of fury and bewilderment. She ignored him and willed Rudy on as she sailed off through the blizzard and out of sight.

'The horse – it's – it's flown away,' the glue man muttered wearily, as if he couldn't quite believe the words he was saying. He grabbed hold of his cart to steady himself.

'I need a mulled wine,' Teddy said, as he struggled to hold Captain Garland upright.

'*Astonishing*,' Captain Garland said. 'Absolutely *astonishing*.'

'YOU,' Mr Krampus growled, his black eyes fixing on Rinki. 'How did you do that?'

'Do what?' Rinki asked.

'Make the horse fly, you silly girl!'

'But horses can't fly, Mr Krampus,' Rinki said cheekily, her eyes still on the sky.

'She's right,' Teddy said with a mischievous giggle. 'You must be mistaken, Mr Krampus. A flying horse? You're seeing things!'

'Then where did the horse go?' he spat.

Rinki, Teddy and Captain Garland stared at him blankly.

Rinki tried to keep a straight face. 'What horse?'

The glue man clutched his head in confusion and sat on the edge of his cart, mulling the whole thing over.

'*You* saw it!' Mr Krampus cried, stabbing at the man's apron with his cane.

'I thought I did,' the man said, blinking through the

snow. 'But it's not possible ... so I must've seen something else.'

Mr Krampus pinched the bridge of his nose in frustration.

'That horse FLEW, and I want to know HOW IT HAPPENED.'

'Goodnight, Mr Krampus,' Rinki said, stealing one last look at the sky.

'THERE IS MORE TO YOU THAN MEETS THE EYE, GIRL, AND I WILL FIND OUT WHAT IT IS!'

Back inside Stratton Street, Rinki headed for the almost deserted kitchen for a quick hot chocolate with Cook. The servants had decorated it with green baubles and big sprigs of mistletoe. The turkey for Christmas Day sat in the corner, dressed and ready for cooking, and a huge Christmas pudding boiled on the stove, whistling steam like it was a festive tune.

Rinki settled herself by the window. *Blanche has found somewhere magic and sent for Rudy. She must've!* she thought. She squeezed her eyes shut and tried to imagine where Blanche might be. She wished with all her might that she could find out.

'I've got no time for magic, as you know,' Cook said, as she plonked a mug of hot chocolate in front of Rinki. 'It's dangerous stuff and it gives me the heebie-jeebies. But I saw what happened out there with Mr Krampus, and even I have to admit, that was nothing short of *satisfying*.'

Mr Krampus stood outside in the snowstorm, staring up at the sky until morning.

He was convinced there was something very strange about Rinki.

Chapter 18

A Surprise Guest

The North Pole was horribly boring.

The Carols' alarm clocks went off at exactly the same time, they dressed in exactly the same clothes and ate exactly the same breakfasts. They spent their days doing exactly the same things – roasting marshmallows on the fire, talking about snow – and at the end of each day they would go to bed in exactly the same pyjamas and turn off their lights at exactly the same time.

Blanche towered over them at the long, icy dining table in the snow in the middle of Carolburg. The elves were discussing the upcoming Snowcus Pocus ceremony, almost reluctantly, as if getting magic were a horrible chore.

'What if one of you wanted to wear different pyjamas?' Blanche interrupted.

'Oh no, that would be *different* and difference is *bad*,' Carol whispered, looking around to check none of the other elves had heard.

'I'm different,' Blanche said. 'Does that make me bad?'

Carol grinned. 'No, you're great.'

'Well, there you go,' Blanche said.

'But difference is bad,' Carol repeated, as if she had rehearsed it many times. Blanche watched with interest as the elf finished her cereal and placed her spoon down at exactly the same time as the other elves.

'I just …' Blanche said, waving her spoon about and making all the Carols wince. 'I don't get it.'

'Look what happened when I did something different,' Carol whispered.

She gestured towards the houses Eggnog had flattened the day before.

'I created a monster. If I had just done what everyone else was doing, things would've stayed exactly the same.'

'But,' Blanche countered, 'if you hadn't made Eggnog, and you hadn't been banished to the floating sheet of ice, you never would have met me. And you say I'm a good thing in your life now, so good *did* come from it. Also, my professional human opinion is that Eggnog is excellent, and possibly the best use of magic I've ever seen.'

Carol beamed proudly, but quickly flicked back to a frown before the other Carols noticed.

'Difference is bad,' she said firmly, as if trying to convince herself.

Then the elves got up, at exactly the same moment, and filed off to their gingerbread houses to take snow showers at exactly the same time.

Later, Carol sneaked off with Blanche to show her the Snowcus Pocus Gallery, where the elves kept their snowmen for the ceremony. They were all exactly the same.

'And I can't remember which Carol made this one,' Carol said.

'Is it because all the snowmen look the same and you're all called Carol and also all look the same?' Blanche guessed.

'No,' Carol said, really thinking about the question. 'I think it's because I'm forgetful.'

'It's always the same,' an elf said later that day. 'Sometimes I wonder what it would be like to eat something other than Candy Cane Chunks for breakfast or chocolate bread for lunch or—'

Blanche decided the moment was right to make a bold suggestion.

'Why don't you all do something different? Something you want to do,' she said with a nervous smile. 'Make a change!'

'DIFFERENT?' the Carols screamed.

'She's a lunatic,' one whispered.

'But I like the name Carol,' another said. 'If we were different, we couldn't all be called Carol!'

'That's – no. You wouldn't have to change your name,' Blanche said. She got to her feet and tried to calm the increasingly jumpy crowd.

'And I like my clothes!' a third cried.

'You don't need to change anything if you don't want to!' Blanche explained. 'What I'm saying is you shouldn't

feel you have to be only *one* way. Difference is good, and the reason you're bored is because you're all doing and saying and wearing the same thing. Imagine if you could tell each other about new things – new ideas, new food, new hobbies. For example, Carol, if you could pick a hobby, what would it be?'

'Being an elf?' Carol guessed.

'That's not a hobby, that's what you are,' Blanche said. 'What sort of things do you like to do?'

Carol looked worried. 'Elf things?'

'I LIKE INVENTING!' came a cry, making everyone gasp. A Carol at the end of the table climbed on top of it. 'I SECRETLY INVENT THINGS WHEN EVERYONE IS ASLEEP, AND I THINK BLANCHE IS RIGHT – WE'D BE HAPPIER IF WE WERE OURSELVES.'

Blanche clapped loudly.

'I LIKE READING BOOKS THAT AREN'T ABOUT CHRISTMAS!' another Carol shouted, making the others gasp again.

'I LIKE USING MY MAGIC TO MAKE HUGGABLE CHRISTMAS TREES!' Carol screamed. 'IT'S NOT SO BAD IF YOU THINK ABOUT IT! IN

FACT, IT'S NOT BAD AT ALL! IT MIGHT ACTUALLY BE *GENIUS*.'

Ripples of excitement spread up the table.

'I LIKE DANCING!'

'I LIKE HUMANS!'

'I LIKE ROLLING AROUND IN THE SNOW NAKED!'

Everyone fell silent.

'Well, that sounds cold,' Blanche said with a cough. She pounded the table with her fist. 'Difference is good – it's interesting and fun!'

The Carols cheered.

A horse flew overhead.

'WHO USED THEIR MAGIC AND FLEW A HORSE HERE?' an elf roared.

Blanche looked across the table to see Carol slowly raise her hand. 'I had to break the rules for Blanche, but now we're allowed to be different, so no floating punishment ice for me!'

Blanche stared at Carol, her mind a muddled mash of excitement and hope and fear that she was wrong. Fear that when she looked up she might not see the thing she wished to see more than anything. The thing that would make her happier than—

'Oh for snowballs' sake, look up!' Carol cried, madly pointing at the horse in the sky.

Blanche raised her chin and blinked back the tears.

'Rudy?' she choked. 'She's really here?'

Rudy's hooves were glowing red and white, but everything else about her was the same – including the disgruntled look on her face.

The horse touched down and spluttered, clearly still somewhat annoyed about the ship incident.

'Oh, Rudy!' Blanche cried, throwing her arms around the horse's neck. 'Carol, how did you know?'

'Once again for the people in the back – I HAVE EARS! I WAS IN THE BOX! I heard you shouting for her, then crying all day and night. Then you told one of my captors about it – the annoying one who bakes … what was his name?'

'Hello?' came a familiar voice.

Blanche turned round. She knew that voice.

'No,' Carol said. 'It wasn't Hello, it was—'

'SANTA!' Blanche cried, tears falling and freezing on her cheeks. His hair was frozen and sticking bolt upright and his clothes were ripped, but he was alive!

'Santa?' Blanche said. He seemed to be swaying on the spot.

Everyone waited for a response, then –

'LOOK AT ME! I'M EXPLORING! I'VE EX-PLORED! POLAR-EXPLORER SANTA!'

Blanche laughed, while Rudy gave a disapproving splutter. She didn't have the context – she had no idea how much Santa wanted to be a brave explorer, and now here he was, looking like someone who had just wrestled a polar bear.

'I said I'd be back, Blanche!' he panted. 'And it's only been –' he looked at his wrist as if consulting a watch. 'I've never owned a watch! Oh, who knows how long it's been, but it's not more than a day or two. Let me see, there was the icy swim, the polar bear thing, a roll through the forest—'

'So you *did* wrestle a polar bear,' Blanche said. 'I thought so from your clothes.'

'The polar bears are our friends!' a Carol said

pointedly. She rolled up her sleeves. 'If I hear that you've hurt one of them—'

'Oh no, I think it just wanted to rough me up a bit,' Santa said with a huge grin. 'And then I ran and tripped over the talking candy cane.'

Blanche raced over and hugged him as hard as she could. Then she turned, ready to introduce him to everyone. But Carol got there first.

'IT'S MY CAPTOR!' she roared. 'HE WAS ONE OF THE MEN WHO ELF-NAPPED ME! HE'S BREACHED THE MAGIC SECURITY OF CAROLBURG! HOW DID HE GET IN?'

'He just sounded so nice,' the security Carol said with a resigned shrug.

Carol blinked furiously, saying nothing.

'Carol,' Blanche said slowly, trying to lay a calming finger on her shoulder. 'Why don't we—?'

'GET THE CAPTOR!' Carol commanded.

A group of elves lunged at him, wrapping him in strings of technicolor icicles until he couldn't move.

Santa shook his head as worried sweat set up home on his brow. The old nervous Santa was back. 'I'm – I'm not a

captor, I swear. I'm just a cook! I've never seen you before!'

'Come on,' Blanche said. 'He's my friend and I promise he's nice. Let him prove it.'

Carol paced back and forth in front of him.

'Fine. What would you like to do to prove yourself to us? What about a joust, or an impossible challenge? Should we call back the polar bear?'

'No!' Santa screeched. 'No, don't do that. I have an idea. I can *bake* something for you. I just need a few ingredients.'

'Are you going to bake *us*?' Carol jeered, whipping up the crowd.

Around her, elves gasped and clutched their hands to their hearts.

'Oh really,' Blanche said, rolling her eyes.

Santa's bottom lip began to tremble. 'I'd never hurt an elf! Also I didn't know you existed until now, so I don't know any recipes that include elves – if there are any, I'm not sure, to be honest …'

Carol clicked her fingers and two elves came running. 'Untie him and get him some supplies. Let's see what the captor can do.'

'She'll warm to you,' Blanche whispered.

'I hope so,' Santa said nervously as he raced off after the elves to the kitchen.

'Just do something simple!' Blanche called after him, but she was shouting at only his footsteps in the snow.

Rudy nuzzled into Blanche. She smelt of sweet carrots, the kind she was fed by the bucketload at Stratton Street.

'Has Rinki been looking after you?' Blanche whispered.

Rudy neighed a yes.

'Rinki,' Blanche said wistfully. She wished she could let Rinki know she was all right. She thought of the snow angels, the wrapping-paper hat, mince-pie picnics, and the plan to give every child in the world a present.

Wait a minute …

'LEAPING CHRISTMAS TREES!' Blanche cried.

'Oh, please don't call Eggnog again,' Carol groaned.

Blanche began pacing back and forth.

Flying Rudy.

The elves.

The magic.

The workshop.

She could make the Christmas plan happen!

She could change Christmas forever.

'I have an idea,' Blanche said. 'And I think you're going to love it.'

'Go on,' Carol said.

'We're going to make next Christmas *magic*,' Blanche promised the elves. 'We can get started the day after this Christmas is done.'

'Oh no,' Carol said. 'I'm afraid the day after Christmas is for being sad and crying about the fact that Christmas – our favourite day – is over.'

'Not this year, Carol,' Blanche said cheerily.

'Maybe we should get the crying out of the way now then?' one of the Carols said.

And with that every single one of them began wailing. Some rolled around on the floor. Some screamed. One of them emitted a strange croak while the Carol next to him squeaked intermittently.

'Well, at least they all cry in different ways,' Blanche sighed. 'It's a start.'

Santa arrived with a jug of hot chocolate. His face fell when he saw the distraught elves.

'What did I miss?'

Chapter 19
Flying Horses

DID YOU SEE THE FLYING HORSE?

*CANDY-CANE STRIPED MAGIC
MAKES HORSE FLY!*

FLYING HORSES: IS DARK MAGIC AT PLAY?

Flying horses became the only thing Mr Krampus would write about in his newspaper, and soon everyone thought he had gone mad. His unbelievable sketches of horses taking off and floating menacingly on clouds didn't help matters. Sales of *The Watcher* newspaper fell to a record low. It was the start of a steep slide in Mr Krampus's fortunes.

People began to point and snigger at him on the street. No matter how loudly he shouted about flying horses and magic, nothing would persuade people that – for once – he was telling the truth.

He blamed Rinki for everything.

And every day he would target her in some way. Sometimes he barged into her in the street, and often he would hamper her hot chocolate plans by buying all the chocolate shavings from the chocolate shop first. But despite his best efforts, Rinki floated about her business with a smile on her face. She was happier than ever, and it infuriated him.

The day before the Costume Society's glamorous Christmas ball, Mr Krampus sneaked through the snow at night and forced open the window of Teddy's study. For days Rinki had been stitching a wrapping-paper trim to a luminous green dress, and she was extremely proud of it.

Moonlight cut through the curtains and fell on the scissors glinting in Mr Krampus's hand. He picked them up and raised them high above his head with an evil grin.

'Say goodbye to your precious creation,' he hissed, before slashing the dress to ribbons.

In the morning, he couldn't resist watching from across the street. He laughed as Rinki cried, clutching what remained of her dress.

A twisted smile curled its way across Mr Krampus's face. 'She'll never be able to make another dress in time,' he whispered to the lamp post.

But that night – the night of the ball – he heard laughter.

He leaned out of his window and couldn't believe his eyes. Captain Garland, Teddy and Rinki were walking through the thick snow towards their house. And Rinki was wearing the green dress! He blinked, convinced he was mistaken.

He watched with fury as she twirled happily.

'You've invented a new look!' Teddy laughed. 'You were the highlight of the ball! Everyone was mad for it!'

'I call it the Krampus Fringe!' Rinki shouted in the

direction of Mr Krampus's house, making him jolt and smack his head on the window frame.

'The girl makes a fool of me at every turn!' he seethed. He vowed that one day, he would know her magic secrets. He vowed that one day, he would make her pay.

Chapter 20

Christmas Eve, Christmas Morning and the Beard

On Christmas Eve, Blanche lay in the snow watching the technicolor lights of Carolburg flicker out until there was nothing but a blanket of starlight.

She could hear the occasional rustle of a wrapping-paper curtain and a tiny elf whisper or two, and even though she was so far from the world she knew, she had never felt more at home.

Suddenly, Carol's face loomed over her, blocking the stars.

'I have a Christmas present for you! But I think

you should open it tonight!'

So Blanche followed her through the snow, past the long ice table and the tiny gingerbread houses, to the very edge of town. There, where the snow flats met the mountains, Blanche could see something large, covered in wrapping paper.

'DON'T LOOK!' Carol insisted, leaping up and covering Blanche's eyes.

She walked on, a little more tentatively now that Carol had her fingers pressed firmly on her eyelids.

'Another step,' Carol said eagerly. 'A-a-and one more.'

Blanche did as she was told and came to a stop. The icy wind howled and she could make out the sound of scurrying feet in the snow.

There was a spluttering neigh, so she knew even Rudy had been roped in for the surprise.

'Don't open your eyes yet,' Carol said as she dropped to the ground and ran off.

Blanche could feel the excitement bubbling in her belly. It took everything in her not to sneak a peek.

'NOW, OPEN THEM!' Carol commanded.

Blanche watched as elves pulled wrapping paper

from whatever it was hiding. The paper whipped around her in torn slivers until every last scrap had settled on the ground and she could see her present.

'CHRISTMAS LODGE!' Carol announced proudly.

Blanche blinked. It looked like a dream – a huge castle of a building, made with gingerbread-men-shaped bricks and snow. Icicles hung from the windows and tree ornaments lined the roof, jingling in the wind.

'Eggnog chose them,' Carol said proudly. 'He wanted to contribute something. Apparently that snowman decoration is his very favourite.'

Each window was trimmed with wrapping-paper curtains and there was an ice-white door with a red bauble knocker.

'For me?' Blanche managed.

'Of course! Just like the one Rinki, Teddy and Captain Garland built for you,' Carol said. 'But with some extra elf flair.'

'It's …' Blanche said, her voice cracking. She tried to blink back the tears.

'Will you stay with us forever?' Carol whispered.

All the elves looked up expectantly, eager to hear her answer.

Blanche looked around – at the elves, at Santa, who was struggling to wheel a huge pot of hot chocolate through the snow, at Rudy, munching on a big pile of elf-sized carrots, and at the magical little town she'd had the good fortune to be dragged to by the ankles. She thought of the bauble and the snowy world she had seen inside it all those years ago as Rinki's voice echoed in her head.

Teddy says you always find your people.

Blanche nodded a yes to Carol, and all the elves cheered.

Turns out my people are mostly elves, she thought, and it made her smile.

Christmas Day with the elves was magical.

The Carols woke her with a huge pile of presents including:

candy-cane striped socks (from Carol)

a warm blanket for Rudy (from Carol)

elf pyjamas (from Carol)

a new Christmas tree-patterned armchair (from
   Carol)

a glittery hairbrush (from Carol)

a gift voucher for snowball fights (from Carol)

and some technicolor icicles (from Carol).

Blanche spent an hour hanging up Christmas cards, all
signed *FROM CAROL*.

The last present she opened was from *her* Carol.

'Just a little gift! I wanted to get you something
unique,' Carol prattled on nervously. 'I want you to
love it.'

'I'm sure I …' Blanche stared at the gift in the wrapping paper.

Carol reached over and lifted it up. It was long, hairy
and white. 'It's for your grand plan!'

'Is it magic?' Blanche asked, holding the limp lump
of hair in her hand.

'Not at all,' Carol said. 'It's to keep your face warm
when you're flying through the sky next year! It's a face
warmer!'

Another Carol held up a mirror for Blanche.

'I asked one of the polar bears if they could spare some of their fur. It'll keep your face very warm. Try it on!'

Blanche looked from Carol, who was beaming with pride, to the strange mass of white hair on her face.

'It looks a bit like a beard.'

'No it doesn't,' Carol said. 'It's a face warmer.'

'Are you sure it doesn't look like a beard?' Blanche asked.

The elves nodded enthusiastically.

Chapter 21

A Classic Christmas Dinner

The Snowcus Pocus ceremony was as weird as Blanche had assumed it would be. She stood with Santa and watched as the elves burrowed into their snowmen, recharged their magic, and then trotted off to get the table ready for the Christmas feast as if nothing had happened.

The long ice table sitting smartly in the heart of Carolburg had been given a festive makeover. Mince pies dangled on strings from huge candy canes dotted along the table between ice candelabras and plates piled high with star-shaped cookies and sweet-smelling stollen. Each place setting had a fat green mug filled with hot chocolate, alongside a little pot of toppings – from gold-flecked marshmallows to candy-cane striped cream.

When Blanche found her place at the table, she discovered her special stocking, the one with the B sewn on it, draped over her seat. Inside was a present from Santa – a notebook, covered with festive wrapping paper and filled with extensive handwritten notes about the different countries in the world and the potential perils Blanche might face in getting a present to every child. Based on information he'd gleaned from sailing the globe, it covered everything from quicksand to mermaids.

Blanche had given Santa an apron with his name sewn in squint letters on the front pocket, and he wore it proudly as he added more and more plates of food to the table.

She thought of Rinki and, in honour of her friend, she took a mince pie, split it in half and raised it in the air. 'Cheers,' she said quietly, smiling up at the sky. She had a feeling that back on a rooftop in London, Rinki might be doing the same.

They were finishing their first course of chocolate soup when the ground began to rumble.

No one noticed it at first, not even Blanche. Santa had just arrived next to Carol with a mysterious covered platter, and Blanche was watching intently to see how it would all unfold. He'd made something extra special to win her over. This was because, while the other elves had been easily persuaded by his delicious baked creations, Carol still insisted on calling him Captor.

'Now, Carol,' he began to explain, 'the other Carols told me you're a big fan of marzipan!'

'No, Captor, I'm not,' Carol said. 'I'm very neutral about marzipan.'

'*Oh*,' an elf nearby said. 'When you said "Carol", I thought you meant *me*.'

Santa looked down at the platter and gulped.

There was another rumble. This time Blanche felt it. She looked round and was sure she saw a rustle in the trees.

'Did anyone feel—?' Blanche started, before deciding against it. She didn't want to ruin Santa's moment.

'I made this especially for you, Carol,' Santa said tentatively, smiling nervously at the elf. 'I hope you like it, it's—'

But he never got to finish the sentence.

'MERRY CHRISTMAS, ELF FAMILY!' came a roar as Eggnog crashed on to the table, sending plates and candles and Carols flying.

The hulking tree then leaped off the table like an overzealous gymnast, causing a huge crack to snake its way through the ice. Blanche watched in horror as the crack charged past her up the table to the very end. The table gave a groan and the whole thing split in two and fell with a thud, flattening Carols on either side.

'MERRY CHRISTMAS, *EVERYONE!*'

Santa's marzipan treat, which had moments earlier been launched into the air, came crashing down on a couple of Carols running in fear. Three houses were demolished as Eggnog excitedly scooped up Blanche into a festive hug.

'WHAT DID YOU THINK OF CHRISTMAS LODGE? DID YOU LOVE THE SNOWMAN DECORATION? IT'S MY *FAVOURITE!*'

While elves desperately tried to free themselves from under the heavy ice table, Eggnog skipped about smashing several more houses, leaving a trail of gingerbread destruction in his wake.

Carol clawed her way out from under the ice table and stood there heaving with rage, her face as red as her hair.

More and more elves emerged around her, removing spoons from their ears and the snow from their mouths.

Eggnog turned. Blanche thought it was entirely possible Carol might burst. Eggnog clearly clocked the strange shade of the elf's face and dropped Blanche to the ground in surprise.

There was absolute silence.

An elf stood bewildered in the rubble, his hair on fire.

'EGGNOG!' Carol roared. 'THIS IS THE LAST STRAW!'

Eggnog gulped.

'Carol's snapped,' one elf whispered to another. 'She's *finally* snapped.'

'YOU ARE TO GO BACK TO THE MOUNTAINS AND NEVER RETURN!' Carol screamed. 'NEEEEEEVEEEEEER!'

'BUT …' Eggnog said, his voice wobbling, 'I JUST WANTED TO BE WITH MY ELF FAMILY … BECAUSE IT'S CHRISTMAS.'

'Look around you, Eggnog!' Carol screamed. 'DOES THIS LOOK LIKE A FAMILY TO YOU?!'

The dinner was ruined, everyone was furious and someone was on fire.

'It actually looks a lot like a family to me,' Santa said as he wiped bits of mince pie from his hair.

'BE QUIET, CAPTOR!' Carol bellowed.

Eggnog's eyes filled with snow tears and he turned to leave, his usual excited bounce now just a sad shuffle.

Casting a desperate look back at Carol, Blanche ran after him. She knew what it was like to feel alone.

'Eggnog, wait!'

The tree turned, his whole body shuddering as tears trickled down his leaves. 'I JUST WANTED TO BE PART OF CHRISTMAS!' he wailed.

'I know,' Blanche said, patting him. 'And I'm going to help you.'

She made a Christmas promise under her breath right there and then that she would find a way for Eggnog to fit in somehow.

One day, he would have his elf family.

Chapter 22

M

After the carnage of the Christmas dinner had been tidied away and all the elves had gone home, Blanche sat down by the fire at Christmas Lodge with Carol and Santa to drink the last of the hot chocolate.

'Adding cinnamon and chocolate sprinkles is INSPIRED, Santa,' Carol said, tipping the cup upside down and letting the last remaining drips trickle into her mouth. 'I *love* cinnamon.'

'*Inspired*,' Blanche mouthed to Santa with a wink.

'Don't think I've forgiven you though, Captor!' Carol added quickly, making Santa's smile tip into a frown.

'I can't wait to get started on our grand Christmas

plan,' Blanche said. It would be a whole year before they put it into action, but she had already begun plotting on scraps of paper – drawings of Rudy flying through the sky, an assortment of chimney designs and a chart of the world's time zones. She wished more than anything she could tell Rinki about it.

'The thing that I don't understand about the plan,' Carol said, 'is how you're going to know what presents the children want. What if you accidentally give them something they already have?'

Blanche thought for a moment. It was a good point.

'We could ask them?' Santa suggested.

'But how?' Blanche said.

Carol rolled on to her back and stared up at the ceiling. 'Hmmm. Ah! Got it. We could send Christmas cards and ask them to reply with what they want.'

'That's a brilliant idea!' Blanche cried. 'Can we do that?'

'Sure,' Carol said casually. 'We'll send the cards via the fireplace in the toy workshop. Any letters posted back will return to the same place. Just keep the return address vague, for obvious reasons – the North Pole should do. The Carols can sort toy requests and assign an elf to fulfil each one.'

Blanche refuelled their hot chocolates and they clinked cups. 'What we start tomorrow is going to change *everything*,' she said, barely able to contain her excitement.

The very next day, Blanche began writing the Christmas cards.

She watched from her window as the elves added the word 'TOY' to the old workshop sign, made with snapped candy canes.

'How should I sign the cards?' Blanche asked.

'What about "FROM THE GHOST OF CHRIST-MAS"?' Carol suggested.

'That's terrifying.'

'What about "BLANCHE"?' Santa suggested as he arrived with some cookies. 'It's your name, after all.'

'Too informal,' Blanche said. 'I think I should sign it simply "*Ms Claus*".'

'I think it'll make them think of CLAWS,' Carol said, holding up her hands like a menacing bear.

Blanche laughed as she signed the card:

Until Christmas,
MS CLAUS

'That's the first one done. Plenty more to go!'

Just then, a Carol arrived carrying a fire poker.

'I'm going to show you how the workshop chimney operates,' he said. 'We'll use the poker to give the cards a good *whoosh*.'

'Soon Ms Claus will be a magical name that makes every child smile when they hear it,' Blanche said. 'Finally the world will see what girls can do.'

'You're an Aries, aren't you?' said another Carol, appearing in the doorway. 'Huge expectations, grand plans ...'

'Carol is really into his astrology and all that stuff,' Carol explained. 'He can read your fortune, if you'd like?'

Astrologer Carol had already eagerly set up a series of charts at Blanche's feet. They were covered in planets and stars.

'I see great success,' he said.

Carol cheered.

'But peril too. Great darkness.'

Blanche swallowed hard. 'Well, that could just be night-time, couldn't it? I do plan to deliver the presents in the dark.'

The elf looked up at her, his eyes wide and worried.

'No, it's not night-time. It's darker than tha—'

Blanche clapped her hands to interrupt him. Everyone jumped. 'It's *fine*. Nothing bad will happen.'

'Let's not get ahead of ourselves,' Carol said. 'There's a chance no child will write back to us …'

Over the next few months, children from Scotland to Australia opened up a tiny glistening card that read:

Greetings!

Soon it will be Christmas, the greatest day of the year. Please write to me at the following address with details of the toy you dream of.

Until Christmas,

S. CLAUS

Toy Workshop
The North Pole

The Carol responsible for sending the cards stared down at the red-hot poker and furrowed his brow. There was a scrap of burnt paper on it.

'M,' another Carol read, peering over his shoulder at it. 'Why are there Ms everywhere?'

They looked around at all the bits of paper that littered the floor. There were thousands of burnt Ms.

'Don't worry about it,' poker Carol concluded with a shrug. 'I think I've been spearing the M off MS CLAUS when I've been pushing the cards up the chimney! It's just an M. Can't imagine it matters!'

But it did. It really did.

Chapter 23
Tinsel

Something had been bothering Blanche. She had written a Ms Claus card for Rinki, so her best friend would know she was safe and putting their plan into action. But she wanted Rinki to be part of it – it was her plan too, and Blanche knew she would *love* it.

She plucked up the courage to ask Carol's permission to use the fireplace mailing system, so she could tell Rinki everything.

Blanche found the little elf in her gingerbread home. All around her were half-made tree ornaments for Eggnog.

'I thought some new decorations might cheer

him up,' she said with a sad smile when she saw Blanche staring at them. 'Since he can't come to town any more.'

Blanche squeezed inside the door and hunched up next to her, tucking her knees up to her chin.

'Carol, I want to write to Rinki and tell her all about where I am and the Christmas plan. Can I use the chimney?'

'Absolutely not!' Carol cried, busying herself with the ornaments again.

'But why not?' Blanche pressed. 'She's my best friend, I'd trust her with anything.'

'It's not Rinki I'm worried about.' Carol frowned. 'What if the letter got into the wrong hands? What if a different human discovered us? One who wasn't as nice as you, or Captor.'

'But none of this would've happened without her,' Blanche protested. 'We're leaving her out of all the fun!'

'No,' Carol said firmly. 'It's too risky.'

Blanche grumbled and squeezed her way back out of the gingerbread house. Outside, inventor Carol was leaning against a neighbouring house, looking shifty.

'Psst,' he whispered. 'I might have a solution to your problem.'

Blanche followed the elf across town to a house. It was almost completely covered in snow and its windows were lopsided. While all the other houses had tiny candy-cane lamp posts outside, this one just had the shattered remains of one.

'Eggnog smashed it,' he said. 'And I stood back and thought – well, it's different to all the others now, isn't it? *Unique*. I thought I'd leave it as it is.'

He chuckled as they ducked inside. Blanche had expected a similarly shabby interior, but it was nothing like that at all. Inside, glittery walls sparkled brightly and the place was so full of gadgets she didn't know where to look. Small candy canes whizzed past her head on beaded string, making her eyebrows change colour as they passed, and ice blocks exploded, sending icy turtle doves flying overhead. In the corner, an angel tree ornament and a toy soldier poured a couple of mugs of hot chocolate.

Blanche squealed with delight. 'You really *do* like inventing things!'

'I do,' the elf said proudly, with a slight bow. 'And I have an invention that will let you tell your friend everything.'

Blanche took a seat on the floor and hoped he didn't mean one of the icy turtle doves, as one had just flown at the toy soldier, practically taking his head off.

The toy soldier marched over, looking a little bewildered, and dropped its cup of hot chocolate in Blanche's lap.

'AAAAAAARGH!' She leaped up, shaking her trousers and wincing at the searing heat.

'CAROL TO THE RESCUE!' the elf screamed. He raced to the window and grabbed fistfuls of snow, formed them into snowballs and threw them at Blanche.

She had to admit the cold helped, though it was strange to be pelted with snowballs and not have a good reason to lob one back.

He then poured another hot chocolate and handed it to her as she sat back down. His hands were shaking, as if his whole body was about to burst with excitement.

'I've never found someone I could help with my inventions before,' he said, reaching into his pocket and pulling out a wad of shimmering paper. He placed it on the floor next to Blanche *very* carefully, as if it might spring to life.

'Let me get a pencil,' he said, rifling through drawers until he found one with a chocolate pudding pattern on it.

'Write something,' he said eagerly. 'Anything! But make sure you address the letter to me.'

Blanche thought for a second and scribbled:

Dear Carol, thank you for the hot chocolate. Love, Blanche.

'Now fold it up and hand it to me!' the elf said, jumping up and down with delight.

She did as she was told and the elf read the letter. When he got to the end, there was a *crack!* and Blanche watched in amazement as the note stretched and shredded itself into a long silvery garland.

'I call it Tinsel.' The elf held it up proudly. 'Not only does it shred after reading, but if anyone else found it, it would shred itself before they could read it.'

He bowed grandly as Blanche clapped.

'So now you can write whatever you want to Rinki, and no one but her will see it.'

'How much tinsel paper do you have?' Blanche asked.

The elf picked up a candy cane and hit the ceiling. Tinsel paper rained down on Blanche until they were up to their necks in it.

'A little bit,' the elf said, in a classic display of elf understatement. 'But I'll get to work on more right away!'

After telling Carol about the tinsel paper and assuring her it worked, Blanche sat down with a mince pie and wrote,

Dear Rinki

I would begin this letter with 'You won't believe this', but I know that of all the people in this world, you will.

It all started with the sinking of the Jolly Holly ...

The letter arrived at Stratton Street via the fireplace in Teddy's study. Luckily Teddy had nipped out to get some

extra sequins. Only Rinki was home – curled up in her reading chair with a book.

The letter shot out and hit her on the nose.

Rinki Greta Garland
6 Stratton Street
London

She ripped it open and stared at the signature in disbelief –

Blanche Claus

As well as the letter, she was surprised to find several sheets of blank paper inside the envelope.

At that moment, Cook arrived with a tray of mince pies. She placed it next to Rinki, who smiled broadly but said nothing.

'Very suspicious,' Cook muttered, because she missed nothing. She straightened a bow on the Christmas tree and left the room, leaving Rinki alone with the letter.

She began to read, and Blanche's adventure made her hug the letter over and over again. She grinned when she got to the bit about Rudy.

When I saw Rudy fly, I knew we could make our plan real. But I think, somehow, you already knew we could. We're going to give every child in the world a present! The elves are so excited – Christmas is their favourite thing.

We're already working to make next Christmas the Christmas we dreamed up at our mince-pie picnic.

'YES!' Rinki roared, punching the air in delight.

We're going to show the world what girls can do, Rinki! I had to write, though Carol is worried that Carolburg will be discovered – it took a lot to convince her to let me. This letter is made out of very special paper, which is designed to self-destruct after reading. It's called Tinsel, and you can use the blank sheets to write back. If anyone else gets hold of it, it'll shred, so our secrets will be safe. You can reach me at the following address:

Christmas Lodge
Carolburg
The North Pole

Until Christmas, when I hope we can have a mince-pie picnic together,

Blanche Claus

As Rinki finished the final line, the letter leaped from her hand with a loud *crack!* and shredded itself.

'Rinki?' came Teddy's voice. 'What was that noise?'

The door opened.

In a panic, Rinki flung the tinsel on to the Christmas tree. She'd told Teddy she would take the tree down, but she didn't want to. Instead she'd been trying to eke it out, taking off one bauble here and another there.

'Rinki?' Teddy said again, waving a hand to get her attention. 'What was that noise? And *what* is that thing on the tree?'

'Oh!' she cried, snapping back to the room. 'The

noise was nothing, and that's tinsel. It's a, erm, *new decoration* from far away.'

Teddy stared at it for a moment. 'That's the opposite of taking down the tree, Rinki. But do you know what? I like it! In fact, I like it so much, let's just leave the tree up all year!'

Chapter 24

Mr Krampus Obsesses over the Claus Cards

Mr Krampus was obsessed with the S CLAUS cards and was determined to find out who had written them.

'THEY CAN'T HAVE ARRIVED BY CHIMNEY!' he had roared at some of the Stratton Street children when they told him. 'IT'S IMPOSSIBLE!'

But while the children were obviously lying about the chimney detail, it was still a feat to be able to deliver cards to *every child in the world*. He knew they were every-where – reports were flooding in from all around the globe.

Who could be rich enough to post so many?

He was determined to be the first to print the answer in *The Watcher*, so he made something up.

PARENTS WRITE LETTERS PRETENDING TO BE MYSTERIOUS S. CLAUS

'What UTTER rubbish,' said Teddy. As indeed did every parent.

The sales of his newspaper, which were already in steep decline, practically dried up after his chimney letter articles. With everything he held dear slipping from his grasp, he grew more and more furious.

That night, he sat in his dark house, gripping his sinister cane.

'This Claus will *not* get the better of me!' he bellowed at the empty room. 'I will find out who he is IF IT'S THE LAST GRUBBY THING I DO.'

Chapter 25

270 Days Left to Get It Right

The plan was in full festive swing.

While Blanche practised riding a flying Rudy through the sky, the elves got busy building and painting the sleigh.

They couldn't agree on the design and so they came up with a selection. One sleigh was made of ice, which Blanche pointed out might be a problem when she got to hotter climates. Another was a gingerbread design, which Santa worried would be potentially hazardous should birds want to eat it. There was one covered in candy canes, which Carol described as 'perilously sticky', one made of cobbled-together Christmas decorations, a terrifying one shaped like a giant elf head, and finally the perfect one.

A simple wooden sleigh painted in a glossy red with a dusting of gold.

Blanche ran her hand over it and inspected the runners. 'I couldn't have dreamed of a better one.'

They fastened the sleigh to Rudy with a special harness, and then she and Blanche took off into the air.

Blanche waved as the elves cheered, but her face fell when she realised something. She came careering down and Rudy skidded to a halt.

'The presents will add weight,' she explained. 'We have to replicate the weight of all the presents.'

Progress had been slow at the toy workshop as the Carols got to grips with saws and hammers, so there weren't enough presents for the experiment. Instead, every elf ran to their house and scooped up their belongings – everything from lamps, candy-cane bed frames and snow-white sofas to bobble hats and hairbrushes.

'Whose are these?' Carol shouted, holding up a pair of platform boots with a heel at least two feet high.

'I just like to feel tall sometimes!' a Carol shouted from the crowd.

Blanche climbed into the sleigh and urged Rudy forward. Just as she'd feared, the poor horse's hooves slipped under her. The sleigh groaned but it didn't budge an inch.

'Come on, Rudy, you can do it,' Blanche said, giving the horse a comforting pat.

Rudy tried again. This time she managed to get some height, but she barely made it above the gingerbread roofs before the sleigh tipped and everything in it tumbled out behind them.

'Well, this isn't good,' Carol muttered.

Blanche could feel the disappointment weighing on her like an overloaded sleigh in the snow. But she wasn't going to give up.

'We need more Rudys,' she said.

Carol nodded and raced off.

It was the first of many stumbling blocks, but neither Blanche nor Santa nor the elves were deterred.

The next day, she opened the door of Christmas Lodge to find something a little different hitched to the sleigh next to Rudy.

'Is that—?'

'It's a reindeer,' Carol said. 'They're about the same size as Rudy and easier to find in these parts.'

'Well, let's try it,' Blanche said, jumping in the sleigh. Elves eagerly lined the take-off route.

'Reindeer are impressively strong,' Carol explained, as Blanche tried to take off. But it was no good, they still couldn't get enough height.

'We need more reindeer,' Blanche said. 'Seven more to make nine – Rinki's favourite number.'

Carol nodded and charged off through the snow towards the mountains, making a squealing sound that Blanche could only imagine was an attempt to communicate with the reindeer.

On the next day of flying tests, Blanche opened the door to Christmas Lodge and found Rudy outside, looking disturbed. There was something spiky on her head.

'Antlers!' Carol cheered. 'I didn't want her to feel

left out. Unlike male reindeer, the female reindeer have antlers at Christmas time, you see. And they were the ones most eager to join the flying squad, so I made Rudy some antlers to match her team of reindeer girls!'

Rudy munched furiously on a carrot, and Blanche knew it was the only thing that was stopping her from eating Carol.

In the evenings, Blanche told the elves she was getting in some extra flying practice, but actually, she'd fly to the mountains to secretly meet with Eggnog. And together they worked on a plan.

'These,' Blanche said, pointing at the tiny stick houses she'd made, 'are the streets of Carolburg.'

'NO, THEY'RE STICKS,' Eggnog said, blowing them over.

'This might take a while,' Blanche mumbled to herself.

Every night they would try to walk around the stick houses without crushing any, like they were learning a dance.

'I CAN'T DO IT, BLANCHE!' Eggnog would cry, and his ornaments would jiggle in frustration.

'YOU *CAN*,' Blanche would say, and she promised him every night she would be there with him until he got it right.

Sometimes Santa joined her – he was the only one who knew about her secret meetings with Eggnog. He would lay out a mince-pie picnic, and together after practice the three of them would sit and drink hot chocolate under the stars.

After Blanche had perfected flying, the next thing to master was what Carol called Chimney Swimming.

'There are hundreds of different chimneys in the world – some thin, some wide, some wonky, some straight – and each has its benefits and pitfalls,' Carol said, as she marched along a line of chimney replicas the elves had carved from ice. The line stretched further than Blanche could see.

'For example, the wide ones are best when you want to get *down*. But they are also the most difficult to climb *up*.'

'No kidding,' said Blanche.

'Take it seriously.' Carol scowled. 'You need to get the timing just right. Morning will be chasing you. If you can beat this obstacle course, you might stand a chance of beating sunrise.'

Blanche stood, poised like a diver, above the first chimney. She felt a wave of nerves as she stared into the frozen chute. She was used to climbing up chimneys, not diving down them. And certainly not replica ones made of ice!

'Ready …' Carol said with a supportive smile.

Blanche nodded and leaned forward.

'Steady …'

Carol held up her stopwatch.

'CHRISTMAS!'

Blanche dived and squeezed and clawed and crawled through ice chimney after ice chimney, before finally collapsing in a wheezing heap when she got to the end.

Carol stopped the clock and frowned. 'At that rate, you'll be able to deliver the presents in … nine days.'

'But I need to do it in one night,' Blanche puffed.

Carol raised the stopwatch in the air once more. 'Then you try again.'

Up and down ice chimneys Blanche went, again and again for months. When she got faster, they added a heavy sack of presents.

'Better?' she panted.

Carol looked at her stopwatch and shook her head. 'You need to be even *faster*.'

Blanche took to running through the mountains at sunrise, pulling Christmas trees tied to her waist behind her. At breakfast, she'd weightlift elves in one hand, while eating her Candy Cane Chunks with the other. After Rinki's letters arrived, she'd use the tinsel as a skipping rope and do pull-ups on the door frame at Christmas Lodge. She trained and trained and went chimney swimming every day, but still her time wasn't fast enough.

'I'M NEVER GOING TO DO IT, AND CHRISTMAS WILL BE HERE BEFORE WE KNOW IT!' she fretted to Santa one night. They sat in the armchairs that flanked the Christmas Lodge fire. Santa was melting marshmallows for their hot chocolate – a little gooey was the trick. He didn't seem to be listening.

'Gooey, gooey,' he said quietly.

Blanche stared up at the ceiling and all the months of frustration came hurtling out of her. 'I CAN'T DO IT!' she yelled over and over again until the gingerbread ceiling wobbled. 'I CAN'T DO IT!!'

'YES YOU CAN!' came a booming voice from outside the window.

There, pressed against the glass, looking slightly smooshed and terrifying, was her favourite enchanted Christmas tree.

'Oh, Eggnog!' she cried as she raced to the door and threw it open. 'You shouldn't be—'

She expected to see flattened elf houses, but there were none.

She leaped into the tree's leafy branches and hugged him tightly. 'You did it! You didn't crush a single house!'

All across town, lights flicked on. Elves popped their heads out of windows and doors and looked around for the damage, just as Blanche had done, then they stared at Eggnog in disbelief.

'HE DID IT!' Blanche cried. 'EGGNOG DID IT!'

The elves began to applaud and cheer.

Carol walked slowly towards him with tears in her eyes.

'You did it, Eggnog,' she whispered. 'I'm so proud of you.'

The praise from Carol made Eggnog bounce with excitement.

'Oh no,' Blanche said. 'Remember, Eggnog, *keep control*.'

Too late.

'I DID IT!' the tree bellowed with such force that the gust knocked Carol backwards into her house.

'TAKE COVER!' an elf screamed as Eggnog tore off through the town, flattening everything in sight.

'I DID IT! I DID IT! I DID IT!'

'He still needs a little work, but hardly any!' Blanche shouted defensively. 'He's almost got it!'

Every day, after every failed chimney-swimming time trial and every delicious meal cooked by Santa and the Christmas Lodge kitchen elves, Blanche would slump in an exhausted heap in her armchair and write to Rinki. And the next morning Rinki would write back. They traded stories of ice chimney obstacle courses and daffodils and summer picnics, reports on the toy workshop and news from costume balls. But the morning after Blanche wrote to her about Eggnog and the wonderful update that he'd walked into town without crushing a single house, Rinki didn't write back. It was strange, given that Rinki loved stories about Eggnog.

Blanche didn't think too much about it – she was busy and Rinki's letters started up again the next day.

It took a long time for them to realise someone else had got to that letter first.

Chapter 26
Stolen Tinsel

Mr Krampus's S. Claus obsession raged on through the summer months. He finished off the headline for the next day's paper – *REWARD FOR PROOF OF THE IDENTITY OF S. CLAUS* – and then turned his attention back to Rinki.

Tormenting her wasn't enough. His reputation was in tatters and he needed to rectify the situation. So he had a rethink.

Magic had made the horse fly, and he knew Rinki was behind it. But he needed solid evidence. Something irrefutable that he could show people. He reasoned she must keep her magic somewhere, and since she was always in that study, perhaps that was a good place to start.

He plotted and planned and waited until Rinki, Teddy and Captain Garland were out of the house – then he paid a visit to 6 Stratton Street.

Cook answered the door and immediately began screaming her jingly bells song. But Mr Krampus had come prepared this time, stuffing some old wrapping paper in his ears to drown out the noise. A servant informed him that Rinki, Captain Garland and Teddy were walking in the park, which, of course, Mr Krampus already knew.

'I'll wait,' he barked. 'And I would prefer to wait *alone*.'

Which was how he came to be in the study with a teacup of mulled wine and a mince pie – alone. He stared down at the mince pie and groaned in disgust. Why couldn't the Garlands just be normal neighbours and put away the Christmas stuff? Where were the summer-appropriate strawberry tarts, for catering's sake?!

He got to his feet and scanned the room, looking for magic. The Christmas tree was still up, of course. He groaned again. Those Garlands!

He flicked through books and looked behind paintings, turned fantastical dresses inside out and lifted rugs. He was ready to give up when something on the tree caught his eye.

He crawled on his hands and knees and grabbed it greedily.

'What strange magic is this?' he said as he watched Eggnog dance inside the bauble.

'This *proves* it. The magic is real, and that girl is the menace behind it!'

He tucked the ice-cold bauble into his coat pocket and grabbed a mince pie, tearing it with his teeth like a beast. He watered it down with some mulled wine and got to his feet.

'Victory!' he said as he staggered to the door in a delirious and delighted stupor. He had one foot out the door when a letter fluttered down the chimney.

Mr Krampus turned quickly on his heel and stared at the shimmering envelope, wondering if perhaps the horrible children had been telling the truth after all.

He popped his head into the hallway to check no one

was around. Then, grinning, he tiptoed back to the fireplace, plucking the letter from the hearth.

Rinki Greta Garland
6 Stratton Street
London

He tore open the letter eagerly. There was a *crack!* and in a flash the letter shredded into a string of tinsel.

He held it up, going cross-eyed with confusion as he tried to understand how a letter could achieve such a feat.

But although inventor Carol's safety measure had kicked in, it hadn't been quite quick enough.

Mr Krampus had caught one word.

Claus.

'Magical letters from Claus?' Mr Krampus said and he began to laugh. 'Of *course* the girl isn't magical – she just *knows* this magical Claus fellow. She's an ordinary girl and I've overestimated her all along.'

He began pacing the room excitedly, and stopped suddenly when an idea came to him.

'I can use her to get to him! Everyone in the *world* will know my name and buy my newspaper! The bauble will *prove* I'm right about magic, and redeem me! And when I tell them whose tree I found it on, Rinki and her precious family will be ruined! Dark magic, I'll call it – everyone will be afraid of them!'

He laughed hysterically to himself.

'That dressmaker will never sell another outfit again. And Captain Garland won't be able to sail! And it'll all be because of that brat Rinki! I'll watch them rot from the inside out!'

Moments later, Rinki, Teddy and Captain Garland were making their way up the front steps when the door flew open and Mr Krampus charged past them without so much as a growl.

'What was he doing here?' Rinki asked the servant in the hallway. 'What did he want?'

'Dunno, miss. He was waiting in the study for you all to come home. Then he started laughing like a maniac and ran off!'

Rinki raced into the study. The reading lamp

illuminated a table displaying a half-drunk teacup of mulled wine and the crumbs of a mince pie. She turned round and round, looking for the reason Mr Krampus had left in such a hurry, but nothing seemed out of the ordinary.

She didn't think to check the ornaments on the tree.

Chapter 27

Blanche Has a Nightmare

Back in Christmas Lodge, Blanche was tossing and turning in her bed as nightmares of melted elves danced through her head.

She sat bolt upright. 'WHAT ABOUT THE HOUSES WITH NO CHIMNEYS?!'

She pulled on her dressing gown and raced out into the snow.

'WHAT ABOUT THE HOUSES WITH NO CHIMNEYS?!' she screamed into the darkness, waking everyone up.

It took Carol, Santa and a couple of extra elves a good half-hour to calm her down, and afterwards they

gathered inside by the fire for an emergency meeting.

'This is Carol,' Carol said, pointing at an elf, 'and while you've been shouting "What about the houses with no chimneys?", he's been doing some no-chimney research for us.'

Blanche stared into the fire, furious at herself for not thinking of it sooner.

'And you've calculated how many houses *don't* have chimneys, haven't you?' Carol said, pushing the Carol with the clipboard forward.

He nodded nervously, a sheen of candy-cane striped sweat covering his brow.

'And how big is this problem?' Carol asked. 'Tell Blanche it isn't as bad as she thinks. How many children don't have a chimney? Five? Ten?'

Clipboard Carol swallowed hard. 'Million.'

'A million?' Carol asked.

'No ... a lot of millions, actually. Many, many millions.'

'What?!' Carol said, grabbing for the clipboard as the other Carol tried to hide it.

'Millions?' Blanche grumbled. 'Great.'

'It's in the millions,' Carol said, clearly hoping there

was a way to make the number sound better than it actually was. 'But on the bright side, it's only about half the houses in the world.'

'HALF?!' Blanche screeched, just as Santa arrived with a tray of hot chocolate – he jumped out of his skin and tipped the whole lot in Blanche's lap.

'The Christmas plan is ruined!' Carol cried. 'AND THE HOT CHOCOLATE HAS BEEN SPILT!'

'I'm so sorry, I'm so sorry, I'm so sorry!' Santa said over and over again.

But Blanche wasn't listening. She stared down at the hot chocolate pooling in her lap and felt giddy.

'The toy soldier spilt hot chocolate on me,' she announced to the group.

'No,' Santa said slowly, holding a hand to her forehead to check if she had a fever. 'I'm *Santa*. Not the toy soldier. SAN-TA.'

'No, I'm fine, really!' Blanche said, laughing. 'You've just given me an idea, that's all. A while ago I went to see inventor Carol and he'd made some Christmas ornaments come to life.'

'I still don't see—'

'If he can do that, then maybe he can bring all the Christmas decorations – baubles, soldiers, angels – to life. Maybe they can open the windows to let the presents in.'

'One snag,' Carol said. 'Something like that would require elf magic. We'll use almost a whole year of magic flying you around the world. The small amount we've allocated as a reserve is for emergencies. If you use it on the houses with no chimneys, then we won't be able to protect you from accidents. We can't keep you safe.'

Great darkness … great darkness. The words of the worried astrologer elf rang loudly in Blanche's memory.

'It's a risk we'll have to take,' she said quickly. 'We can't have half the children missing out – it's all of them or none of them.'

And so the next day, inventor Carol sewed the extra elf magic into an elf-style hat.

'The white pom-pom at the end holds the magic,' he explained. 'Shake it and toys and tree ornaments will come to life inside the house.'

Blanche pulled on the hat, it was floppy and the pom-pom dangled in her face. 'It's perfect,' she said. '*And* it'll keep my head warm!'

Chapter 28
Eyes on Rinki

Teddy's designs were more popular than ever, and Stratton Street now looked like a catwalk, with a continuous procession of people filing out of number 6 with smiles on their faces and garment bags on their arms.

Rinki began helping Teddy with the fittings – pinning and sewing and creating her own designs – and sometimes she would sit and read aloud from her favourite books to entertain the customers.

But underneath it all, something was bothering her. What on earth had Mr Krampus been doing in the study? It had been two days, and the fact he hadn't made any sort of sinister move was putting her on edge.

That day, the department store was revealing Teddy's limited collection, so Rinki went to see the designs in the shop window.

'Rinki designed many of these,' Teddy explained, and it was true. Everyone loved the designs with her Krampus Fringe.

Normally, seeing her designs in a real shop window would be a dream come true. And to know that Blanche was fulfilling her wildest dreams as well should have made her happy. She tried so hard to be happy, but everything felt increasingly tainted by the spectre of Mr Krampus. She half expected him to be lurking behind her, wielding scissors or his horned cane, just because he could.

On her way home from the department store that day, she had a horrible feeling she was being followed. But when she whipped round, there was no one there.

It was all getting too much. She hated feeling so scared, and so she decided to take herself somewhere that reminded her of the stuff she was made of. She poured herself a mug of hot chocolate and walked all

the way to the corner where Christmas trees were sold.

It was summer and not the time for Christmas trees, but the corner wasn't deserted. A young man stood there selling newspapers.

'Out for a stroll with some hot chocolate?' he asked.

'Something like that,' Rinki muttered as she stared fondly at the spot in the road where she and Blanche had had their first mince-pie picnic.

Leaping Christmas trees!

To show we'll be friends for as long as we wear them.

Rinki looked down at her gold thread ring and felt fierce again.

'You heard about the magic?' the boy said, thrusting a *Watcher* newspaper under Rinki's nose. The headline read:

NO ORDINARY BAUBLE – MAGIC OBJECT
FOUND IN LONDON

Gather at Stratton Street at 3 p.m. today to see the magic bauble and watch as the dangerous demon behind the magic is revealed!

Rinki's mug of hot chocolate slipped from her hand and smashed to the ground. She ran home – straight to the tree.

'No, no, no, no, no, no, no!' she cried.

Her hands shook uncontrollably as she pulled every decoration off the branches.

Blanche's special bauble was gone.

'Oh!' Teddy said as he passed by the doorway. 'You're finally taking the tree down!'

Rinki barely registered his comment and he carried on to the kitchen. She reached for some blank tinsel paper, but thought better of it and scrunched it into a ball.

The last thing Blanche needed was another problem to worry about. Rinki decided she would deal with Mr Krampus herself.

She plucked a plain red bauble from the pile of decorations.

She had an idea.

Rinki landed with a squelch, her sequined boots sinking fast in Mr Krampus's muddy flower bed. She crunched

her way over dead plants to the back door and used a hairclip to pick the lock.

Inside, she met with a long dark corridor that snaked off into the distance. She could hear Mr Krampus stomping about downstairs in the kitchen, so, with her heart beating so hard she thought it might catapult out of her mouth, Rinki cracked open the door to his study.

Slivers of weak sunlight squeezed through the gaps in the closed curtains, striking a desk in the middle of the room.

And right in the middle of the desk, sitting like a sacred treasure in a dark cave, was the bauble.

Quick as lightning, she grabbed the real one and swapped it for the red bauble in her pocket. She was about to run when she was distracted by something jammed in the desk drawer. Something shimmery and familiar.

'It can't be,' she said with a gasp when she pulled the drawer open. A shredded tinsel letter was lying inside.

Beside it on a notepad, Mr Krampus had written, *But who is Claus?*

Mr Krampus knew she was connected to Claus! She began to sweat. His two obsessions tangled into one!

A door banged down the hall, making Rinki jump.

With only moments to think, she shoved the drawer closed and skidded across the room, tucking herself behind the curtains just in time.

An old grandfather clock chimed three o'clock.

The door to the study flew open and Mr Krampus stomped in.

Rinki held her breath. She didn't dare look.

The footsteps stopped. Rinki squeezed her eyes tight shut.

'COME ON, MR KRAMPUS!' came a shout from the crowd gathered outside. 'SHOW US YOUR MAGIC BAUBLE THEN!'

Rinki began to shake, terrified he would come to the window to shout back. But she was in luck – Mr Krampus's footsteps disappeared out into the hallway.

This was her chance. She reached up and unhooked the window locks, pulling the sash with all her might. It was heavy and creaked terribly. She knew she only had seconds to play with.

The warm summer air flooded in and she threw herself out of the window. She landed with a crunch near the waiting crowd and dusted herself off.

Moments later, Mr Krampus flung open his front door and held up the bauble.

'*MAGIC*,' he said grandly.

The crowd shuffled closer.

'SEE THE DANCING CHRISTMAS TREE INSIDE.'

Ripples of laughter began to spread through the crowd, and soon the whole audience was in hysterics.

'What's so funny?' Mr Krampus grumbled, taking a moment to look in the bauble.

When he understood what had happened, he turned quite pale with fury. Then he spotted Rinki in the crowd.

'GIRL!' he growled. 'I WILL DESTROY YOU *AND* YOUR FRIEND CLAUS!'

Chapter 29
The Toys

It was autumn, and December was fast approaching. All year long the elves had been busy in the workshop hammering and soldering and painting the millions of toys needed for Christmas Day. The letters from children had come thick and fast – flying through the fireplace and magically sorting themselves into piles. Train sets, dolls, marbles, board games, the list was endless.

Rinki hadn't requested a toy. On the card she had simply written:

I don't need a toy, but I would love a mince-pie picnic with Blanche.

'DON'T KNOW HOW TO MAKE THIS ONE!' an elf shouted, waving the letter.

The elves were new to making toys so there had been some bumps along the way.

Blanche had appointed inventor Carol as the head toymaker – she liked his can-do attitude.

Although many of the toys were already made, there was still a lot to do. Blanche's Carol was keen to help, so she pitched in with the trains team.

'I've finished my first one!' she cried as soon as Blanche stepped into the toy workshop.

It was instantly apparent that there was a problem with Carol's train design.

'Um,' Blanche said, as she stood beside the full-size engine – it was so big she could fit in it comfortably with room to spare. 'Carol, this is beautiful, but what do you think might be wrong with it?'

'THERE'S SOMETHING WRONG WITH IT?!' Carol screamed. She didn't like making mistakes. She pulled nervously at her collar. 'Is it the wrong colour? You wanted blue and I've given you green!'

'No,' Blanche said softly. 'It's not the colour.'

'I know!' an elf at the back shouted, waving his hand in the air.

'It's too shiny?' Carol guessed again, inhaling a mince pie to soothe her nerves.

'No, it's impressively shiny,' Blanche said.

Santa arrived with hot chocolate for the elves. 'Wow, that is a HUGE train!'

Carol's face fell. 'What? It's *big*, that's what's wrong with it? BUT I'M AN ELF! EVERYTHING IS BIG TO ME!'

'Exactly,' Blanche said, trying to make things better. 'That's why you're perfect for making toys – just make everything elf-sized.'

'*Oh!*' Carol said. '*I see.*'

Blanche sent a tinsel letter to Rinki, asking for some help with dress designs for the dolls:

The elves mostly wear green, and they don't get much inspiration looking at me in my carter trousers and shirt.

It didn't take long for Rinki to send back two beautiful designs.

Dear Blanche,

I loved designing these! I made one doll a fringed green dress, like the one I wore to the costume ball, and the other a silver smock with a sky-blue cape. I really hope you like them!

But as time ticked on, Blanche started to notice that Rinki's letters were becoming increasingly short. It felt as if Rinki was trying to distance herself from the plan – and from her. She lay in bed at night worrying she had done something to upset her.

Chapter 30
Time to Tell Blanche

Rinki couldn't shake the feeling Mr Krampus was watching her.

As the days and weeks passed, she felt her worries beginning to engulf her. She caught glimpses of eyes watching her in crowds, and every time she passed Mr Krampus's house, she was sure she could see him peering through the gaps in the curtains.

Even though the iron box was empty, the strange men in suits lingered too, staring at her from their spot across the road.

Rinki lay in bed one night and thought of Mr Krampus's cane carved with a thousand eyes. She could see it in the darkness, floating above her bed, the eyes blinking over and over and over again. The wind howled as it raced down the chimney, and though she tried with all her might not to be, she still felt scared.

She had tried to protect Blanche from as much of this as possible, but Mr Krampus knew too much, and now Rinki had to tell her he'd uncovered the link between them. Blanche was in danger too – and it was time she knew it.

Chapter 31

Cancel the Mince-Pie Picnic?

'Well, I'm just going to say it,' Santa said when Blanche read Rinki's Mr Krampus letter aloud at Christmas Lodge. 'It's by *far* the worst thing I have ever said, but Mr Krampus is *MOULD*.'

'Mould?' Carol scoffed. 'That's the worst thing you've ever said?'

'Mould causes irreparable damage to baked goods, Carol! Mould is very bad.'

Carol tried not to laugh.

'And …' Santa struggled, as if trying to squeeze unwilling words out. 'He's so … very … UNPLEASANT.'

Carol clapped. 'You get that fury out, Captor. I've never heard such terrible words.'

Santa looked delighted with himself.

Blanche began to pace the room. She felt as if everything was falling in on her, like a gingerbread house trampled by Eggnog. She still had to beat sunrise and there were only a few days left before Christmas Eve – she couldn't let Rinki and the children down. And now she had to worry about Mr Krampus as well.

'He's closing in on us,' Blanche said gravely.

'You must not have the mince-pie picnic,' Carol commanded. 'Not this year. It's too risky.'

But when Blanche reluctantly wrote to suggest cancelling, Rinki's response came clattering down the chimney as determinedly as the note inside.

Blanche, every time you write, I remember that we can do anything – separately or together.

I will not live my life differently because Mr Krampus has decided to tangle himself in it. I'm tired of being scared. We WILL have our mince-pie

picnic, because it is ours and no one will take it
away from us.

'Well, if you're determined to do it, then make sure he's asleep when you arrive,' Carol said. 'He'll be watching Rinki very closely on Christmas Eve – to see if she leads him to you.'

'Could we use elf magic?' Blanche asked.

'We're not made of magic!' Carol cried. 'If you want to cancel your plan for getting into houses without chimneys, that would give us a lot of extra magic to deal with Mr Krampus.'

'No, no,' Blanche said. 'The houses without chimneys are more important. We'll have to think of something else.'

Leave Mr Krampus to me, Rinki wrote. *I'll come up with something.*

Chapter 32

The Brussels Sprout Brew

'Hot chocolate coming up! You don't even have to ask!' Cook announced as Rinki stepped into the kitchen.

'Actually, I didn't come for hot chocolate,' she said, making Cook's jaw drop. 'I was hoping you might be able to help. Teddy said you know all sorts of wild, old recipes. Maybe even a recipe to put someone to sleep?'

'Sleeping brews?' Cook said, thrashing around the kitchen for hot chocolate ingredients anyway. 'Even if I did have recipes like that – and I *don't* – I wouldn't have time to make them!'

'What if I said it was for Mr Krampus?' Rinki

said. 'What if I really needed him to be asleep on Christmas Eve?'

Cook stirred the milk on the stove and didn't say a word. She poured it into Rinki's mug and then dropped in shavings of chocolate. 'Mr Krampus you say,' she eventually said. 'This hasn't got something to do with the suspicious amount of tinsel around here, has it?'

'It might,' Rinki whispered.

Cook hurried over to a picture on the wall – a watercolour Teddy had painted of festive food. He'd called it *The Christmas Lunch Club* and had given it to Cook as a present.

Behind it was a hollow space containing half a burned book.

'Recipes!' Cook said, holding it up. 'My most treasured possession.'

Then she set it down carefully on the table. Rinki could just make out a name scrawled on the curling front page.

'Befana,' Rinki said, tracing the letters with her finger.

'It's been in my family for hundreds of years,' Cook explained. 'I learned everything I know from this book.

They say Befana was a witch and she was burned with this book. My great-great-great-great-great-great-grandmother was her best friend, and she found what remained of the book in the ashes. It's been passed down the generations ever since.'

'Why was she burned?' Rinki dared to ask.

'Because they said she was a witch, and that just means she annoyed a man at some stage.'

Rinki leaned closer. 'Maybe she really was a witch!'

Cook flicked through the pages, saying nothing.

'But you always say you hate magic,' Rinki said. 'And yet you have a book that once belonged to a woman who was thought to be a witch.'

'Of course I say I hate magic!' Cook cried. '*Because* of the book. I don't want them bringing back the whole "Let's accuse women of being witches when we don't like them!" thing. At least my defence would be, "I'm not one of them – check with anyone. I *hate* magic – gives me the heebie-jeebies."'

She paused at a page and passed the book over.

Rinki examined the page Cook had presented her with.

BRUSSELS SPROUT BREW

For sweet slumber

Rinki smiled. 'Perfect!'

They got to work.

The Brussels sprouts had to be stewed and squashed before a Yuletide bouquet of cinnamon, cloves, nutmeg and sage was added.

The stench became so overwhelming that Cook ran to the laundry room and returned with clothes pegs for their noses.

Next was a jar of cherries and a sprinkle of fig shavings, which turned the mixture black.

'An egg,' Cook read. 'To make it glossy.'

Then came a clump of dust.

Then a little kiss.

'You kiss it,' Cook said.

'No, you!' Rinki insisted, before relenting and kissing the hideous gloop.

'And stir,' Cook said, handing Rinki a big spoon. As soon as she stirred it, all the ingredients combined to create a lurid green slop.

'Bottle and store,' Rinki said, putting the book aside. 'Keeps in the larder for up to a year!'

Cook handed her a milk bottle and Rinki ladled the liquid into it.

'Now we have to figure out a way to get him to drink it,' Rinki said, removing the clothes peg from her nose. 'That'll be the tricky bit.'

'That will be easy, my dear!' Cook said, putting the book back behind the painting. 'He hires a cook for his Christmas Day feast – says he hates Christmas but he eats all the food! They arrive on Christmas Eve to prepare it. He always makes them cook a meal for him that night too. I'll make sure that when the time comes, whoever is cooking has this bottle, Rinki. On Christmas Eve, he'll drink it and you won't see him again until Boxing Day.'

Chapter 33
Running Out of Time

By October, Rinki's room had grown so full of tinsel the door bulged when she closed it. She'd stuffed it in stockings and under her bed, but more letters kept coming and more tinsel kept flourishing until she had to swim through it to get to bed.

'What is going on in there?' one of the Stratton Street servants had cried.

'Nothing,' Rinki said, as she stood flat against the door, her arms stretched out wide. Tinsel was escaping around the edges of the door, and the servants knew *something* was going on, they just couldn't figure out *what*.

In November, the door to Rinki's bedroom had flown right off and she'd had to store the tinsel on the roof. The pile had grown and grown, until in early December, 6 Stratton Street drew crowds from miles around, marvelling at the festivity of it all.

But by the 23rd of December, Blanche's replies to Rinki's letters had almost stopped.

In Carolburg, Blanche had been training harder and faster every day – adding more and more elves to her breakfast weightlifting. Now she was running with Eggnog, the heaviest tree in the forest, tied to her waist.

'YOU CAN DO IT!' he cheered happily as she pulled him through the snow. 'YOU CAN MAKE CHRIST-MAS!'

For one final time, Blanche stood poised above an ice chimney, staring out at the frosty obstacle course that stretched further than she could see.

'You know, Blanche,' Carol said in a voice that Blanche knew was designed to soothe her. 'You could start with *half* the world and work up to the *whole* world in a couple of years.'

Blanche refused to consider the option – every child had got her letter, so every child had to get their present. It was as good as a promise and she couldn't break it.

'Well,' Carol said, raising the stopwatch in the air, 'tomorrow you fly. So this is it – your last chance.'

That evening Blanche dived down and crawled up and squeezed through and wriggled around the line of ice chimneys one last time, pushing herself like she'd never pushed herself before. She heard the familiar click of Carol's stopwatch at the end, expecting the usual 'Not quite quick enough', but there was only silence.

Blanche wiped the sweat from her brow.

'I feel like we're close, but it's that bendy one. Maybe there's time for one more quick practice. If I can just swing my left leg and do the drop a couple of seconds faster—'

She turned to see Carol holding the stopwatch in her face.

'You did it,' Carol squeaked in awe. 'You beat sunrise!'

That night, a present from Rinki arrived, wrapped in tissue paper and sealed in a gold box.

The elves and Santa gathered round as she opened it.

Merry Christmas, Blanche! You forgot something in your plan –

Rinki wrote,

– something fabulous to wear.

Blanche pulled the garment from the box.
It was the beautiful red suit with the ice-white trim.

Chapter 34
It Worked!

'**B**RUSSELS SPROUTS!' came a roar from outside Rinki's door.

It was just after dinner on Christmas Eve and she was tucked up in bed reading when Cook flung open the door, causing a tidal wave of tinsel to spill out into the hallway.

'It's Mr Krampus,' she said. 'He drank the brew!'

They tore downstairs to find Mr Krampus skipping up and down the lamplit street. A green stain circled his mouth and he was shouting gleefully, listing the ingredients.

'Cinnamon! Nutmeg!'

He tried to hug a passing woman and was promptly shoved face first into the snow.

'FIGS!' he bellowed, getting back on his feet. 'AN EGG!'

'He seems very awake …' Rinki whispered, just as he collapsed in a heap and began snoring.

Cook raced out and lifted him up. 'Come on, Mr Krampus,' she said, giving Rinki a wink. 'Let's get you tucked into bed.'

Rinki closed the front door and slid down it in relief. Maybe, just maybe, the Christmas plan was saved.

But the problem with Mr Krampus and his hideous cane was that he had made Rinki and Blanche underestimate everyone else.

Chapter 35
Sleigh Bells Ring

Christmas Eve in the North Pole was very different to Rinki's Christmas Eve in London.

In order to make sure Blanche was beating sunrise, the Carols had built a giant red bauble – an illuminated orb showing every inch of the Earth – to track the sleigh around the world.

'Then we can let you know if you're keeping to time,' Carol said as Blanche inspected a long list of numbers.

'We'll attach this to Rudy's nose,' Carol said, holding up an identical but much smaller red bauble. 'We'll use it to talk to you and see where you are – think of it as a crystal ball, but in real time. I was inspired by the red bauble you're always going on about!'

'Thank you, Carol,' Blanche said. 'I think Rudy really suits a red nose.'

Rudy spluttered, because *she* did not.

'And whatever you do, don't break the bauble. If you do, we'll be out of contact – if something bad happens and the bauble is broken, I'm afraid you're on your own.'

Blanche thought back to astrologer Carol. His voice echoed in her head, *Great darkness … great darkness … great darkness.*

Blanche turned to Santa. 'I can take you home,' she said, gesturing to the sleigh.

'Home?' Santa said.

Blanche nodded. 'London! I can drop you off.'

Santa's face crumpled and he looked as if he might cry.

'NO!' Carol roared, grabbing hold of Santa's leg.

'No?' Blanche said, with a raised eyebrow. 'I thought he was a captor and a villain?'

Carol let go, clearly annoyed with herself for losing

her composure. 'He is. I just, well, he's not that bad and I would like it if he stayed.'

'I'd like to stay too!' Santa said, beaming down at her. 'I love cooking for all my new friends and I can't imagine living anywhere else now.'

'PHEW!' an elf said. 'We've been stockpiling mince pies in case you left. We even tried to make our own, but Carol set his ear hair on fire.'

'I did not!' the only Carol with black ear hair cried, crossing his arms angrily. 'Maybe I dyed it.'

'Well, here goes!' Blanche said as she climbed into the sleigh. 'This is the Christmas that will change everything!'

Behind her, the presents were piled high.

She gathered the reins, unable to believe that the moment was finally here. She felt thrilled and sick and jolly and terrified, all at the same time.

The elves crowded around her.

'Merry Christmas, Blanche,' Carol said with a proud smile.

'Merry Christmas, Carol.'

Blanche looked to the mountains to wave goodbye

to Eggnog, but he was busy rolling down the mountainside in a wave of snow.

'Eggnog is starting avalanches again,' Carol groaned.

'AND HE'S NAKED!' another Carol screamed, spotting he wasn't wearing any of his decorations.

'For Christmas's sake, Eggnog!' Carol shouted. 'PUT SOME DECORATIONS ON!'

'Don't forget this,' Santa said, handing Blanche a flask of hot chocolate and a stocking full of snacks. 'For the journey. I've included all your favourites.'

Blanche smiled and placed the stocking and flask under her seat. She gripped the reins and gritted her teeth. 'Tally—'

'Don't forget your face warmer!' Carol interrupted, climbing up and fixing it on Blanche's face. She patted it down to make sure it was *really* secure.

'You're sure it doesn't look like a beard?' she asked, the white fur getting in her mouth as she spoke.

The elves shook their heads.

Santa frowned. 'It does look a bit like a—' But Carol kicked his leg before he could finish.

'It doesn't matter what it looks like,' she whispered. 'What's important is that it keeps her face warm.'

Blanche took a deep breath and tried to settle her nerves. Rudy glanced back from the front of the herd and winked. It was a glance she often gave her before they set off on their cart, and Blanche felt braver because of it. Carol had made Rudy a glittering nametag attached to her harness, and each reindeer had one too. It suited Rudy, Blanche thought. And so did the gleaming sleigh.

'We picked the reindeer's names out of an elf hat,' Carol explained. 'And I made them all tags so you don't forget them! I'm so relieved we got things like Blitzen and Comet and Cupid. Some elves have *toilet humour*, and let's just say you could've been shouting out some *disastrous* words if they'd had anything to do with it.'

Blanche laughed and tried to settle her nerves once more.

'Enough stalling,' Carol said, tapping her clipboard. 'It'll soon be Christmas Day and you, Blanche Claus, have places to be.'

Blanche thought of the Christmases when she'd longingly watched carriages dancing along the icy

streets, wishing she had somewhere to be. Well, now she did – she had everywhere to be.

'TALLY-HO!' she cried, louder than she had ever cried it before.

And with that, Rudy and the reindeer took off into the starlit sky.

They soared high over the North Pole, cold snowflakes pricking at their cheeks and icy winds whipping them sideways. Blanche had added bells to their antlers and they jingled as the sleigh soared above the first houses, heading south.

She flew high over mountains and coastlines, through the clear, starry sky, then through rain, sleet and blizzards so thick Rudy and the reindeer disappeared behind a blanket of white. She tore over tiny towns and sprawling cities and villages perched on clifftops.

The world was magical – every inch of it.

She landed with a clatter, slipping down chimneys and tiptoeing around houses. She walked past twinkling Christmas trees dressed in baubles and bows and scooped up milk and cookies and carrots that the children had laid out for her.

On the rooftops of houses without chimneys she shook her hat and little Christmas decorations would open the windows. Blanche watched as soldiers, teddies, angels and rolling baubles carried presents to Christmas trees and stockings.

At one house she slipped on the snow, shaking the hat so violently that it didn't only bring the Christmas decorations to life but every toy in the street. Blanche lost some time negotiating with hundreds of teddies and dolls smooshed at every window, insisting they be the one to help her.

Despite the mishaps she was making good time, but sunrise was always behind her, inching closer.

As she flew over London, she felt wobbly with excitement. Rinki and a mince-pie picnic were moments away.

She made a quick stop at the docks first, landing on the old stone tack hut and making her way down the chimney.

Whipper, Cole and Sprout were fast asleep, huddled in the corner for warmth. She had promised every child would get a gift, and no matter what they had done, the carter boys were no exception. She carefully lined up their presents around the fireplace and, just before she climbed back up the chimney, she added some of the goodies the children from other homes had left her – cookies, bottles of milk and chunks of chocolate.

She didn't notice, but behind her, Whipper opened an eye and watched.

He recognised her instantly.

He knew the secret.

Chapter 36
Real Magic

Rinki was waiting on the roof of 6 Stratton Street, waving both hands with delight as Blanche landed with a soft crunch on the snowy roof.

The friends threw their arms around each other.

'Look at you,' Rinki said, holding Blanche's face in her hands. 'You look so glamorous!'

'It's the suit,' Blanche said with a grin. 'Thank you for sending it. Does Teddy know our secret plan?'

'I'm sure he's guessed. He saw Rudy flying that first time, and so did Jolly. And I had to tell them you weren't dead and that I've been sending you things – Teddy let me have the suit.'

'It does add something,' Blanche said, doing a little twirl.

'I think it was always meant for you,' Rinki said. 'Now come on, we mustn't waste any time. Let's have the mince-pie picnic and you can tell me how tonight is going so far.'

'Is it safe?' Blanche said, peering over the edge and expecting to see Mr Krampus and his creepy cane. All the houses were dressed in their festive best, apart from Mr Krampus's house. It stood dark and dangerous in the middle of Stratton Street, like a gaping hole in the heart of Christmas.

'Don't you worry, Blanche, that old groan is out for the count. If you listen hard, you can hear his snoring.'

Back in the North Pole, the elves circled the huge red bauble, watching the clock nervously as Blanche and Rinki laughed and cried, ate mince pies and argued over the best way to consume them. Blanche picked off the crust carefully before devouring the contents, whereas Rinki ate them in one. The elves copied the different techniques and concluded that Rinki's was better – you could get through more mince pies that way.

'Don't worry, she's making good time,' Carol said, marching back and forth as she checked the progress chart. 'Let them have their mince-pie picnic.'

From the roof, Blanche could see the strange men in suits standing in the shadows across the street.

'They're still here then?' she said to Rinki.

Rinki nodded. 'I left the iron box in the window – open – so they could see there's nothing inside it any more, but they still haven't gone.'

She reached into her pocket.

'Here's something else that hasn't gone away.'

She pulled out Blanche's red bauble.

'I've kept it with me ever since Mr Krampus tried to steal it, but you can have it back now.'

Blanche cupped it in her hands – it was still as cold as ice. She peered into it and saw Eggnog, dancing happily in deep snow.

'Eggnog,' Blanche said wistfully. She handed the bauble back to Rinki. 'You keep it here. One day when the time is right you can pass it on to a child who needs it, just like it was passed on to me.'

'I will,' Rinki said with a fond smile. 'I wonder what destiny it will show its next owner. Because that's what it did, didn't it? I was right all along. Although I was wrong about you becoming a tree.'

Blanche laughed. 'I've thought about it *a lot* and I think it showed me what was possible – that's the bauble's magic, and the wisdom of the old woman who thought to pass it down to me.'

Blanche lay flat on her back, staring up at the snowy sky.

'When you really think about it, it's the non-magic moments that really changed things – crashing into you, finding Rudy, mince-pie picnics on rooftops. It's the small and ordinary things that snowball to make a life truly magical.'

Rinki squeezed her hand.

'This bauble made me believe that sometimes it only takes one day to change everything.'

Rinki raised her mince pie. 'To Christmas!' she said.

Rudy neighed and the reindeer gave a collective celebratory splutter.

Blanche watched as Rinki stared at the sleigh.

'I wish you could come back and live with me, Rinki.'

Rinki smiled sadly. 'I would love to visit you, but I couldn't leave Teddy and Jolly and my home – my life is here.' She raised her pinky finger displaying her gold thread ring. 'But I'm always with you.'

Blanche got to her feet and dusted the snow off her suit. She held out her hand to Rinki. 'I can't leave without taking you for a spin.'

And so off they went. Rinki held her arms in the air as they soared across the park and over her favourite statue. They glided low along the frozen river and then shot up into the sky, back towards Stratton Street.

'Sunrise is catching up,' came Carol's voice from Rudy's red nose. 'Time to go. And, Santa – get me a hot chocolate! We're on the home stretch!'

Blanche reluctantly landed on the roof, and Rinki hopped out.

'Until next Christmas,' Blanche said, lingering a little longer.

'Until Christmas,' Rinki said with a smile. 'Now go!'

Chapter 37

Mr Krampus Wakes Up

As Blanche got ready to leave Stratton Street, two things of crucial importance happened, though on their own they were of little importance at all. The first was that Santa arrived with the hot chocolate for Carol. The second was that the Brussels Sprout Brew had worn off earlier than expected and Mr Krampus had stirred from his sleep.

As Blanche turned and waved goodbye to Rinki, Mr Krampus made his way to the window, and Santa made his way towards Carol with the hot chocolate.

When Mr Krampus drew back his curtains, he saw a figure in the distance – a figure flying on a sleigh pulled by reindeer in the sky. Meanwhile, in the North Pole, at the *exact* same moment, Santa tripped and spilt the hot chocolate all over Carol, who screamed in surprise and kept on screaming.

Irritated by what was happening at the end of her nose, Rudy began trying to shake off the bauble, dragging the sleigh into a perilous downward spiral.

They were out of control.

Moments later, Blanche fell.

With one hand she managed to grab the sleigh's edge, her knuckles seizing up as she tried to hang on.

'Sorry about that,' she could hear Carol saying. 'The Captor spilt hot chocolate all over me!'

'Who are you?' Mr Krampus whispered, looking up at the dangling figure in the sky. Which was unfortunate, because at that exact moment, upon hearing about the hot chocolate fiasco, Blanche shouted –

'SANTA!'

Finally, Rudy righted the sleigh and Blanche clambered back into it. She gathered up the reins and took off, completely unaware that Mr Krampus was watching and incorrectly piecing things together.

The Christmas card signed 'S CLAUS' …

The mysterious person with the flying sleigh who when asked for a name replied 'Santa' …

On Christmas morning, Mr Krampus spotted something glinting in the snow outside his house – half a nametag, dropped from the sky.

RUD it said, the remainder of the name broken off.

He grinned and stuffed it in his pocket.

Chapter 38
The Mistake

On Christmas Day, the elves were so exhausted they struggled to burrow into their Snowcus Pocus snowmen.

Blanche slept through the whole day and the day after that, before being woken by Carol with a stack of newspapers.

'LET'S SEE WHAT THE WORLD IS SAYING!' Carol said, wiggling with excitement.

Blanche had expected to see headlines about presents delivered by a mysterious girl flying through the air. Unfortunately *The Watcher* was the only paper that had run a story at all.

And the headline made Blanche rage.

'THEY THINK I'M A MAN CALLED SANTA CLAUS?'

'It'll never catch on,' Carol assured her.

The next day was worse. The other newspaper reporters had no idea who had delivered the presents, but dozens of them had run *The Watcher*'s Santa story. A man had reported a magical sleigh being pulled by reindeer flying through the sky, driven by a Mr Santa Claus.

Blanche read on.

'*When the man asked the mysterious Claus his name, he told him he is called Santa.*'

'That didn't happen!' she said. 'What happened was that I shouted Santa when he spilt the hot chocolate on Carol. I was over Stratton Street and Mr Krampus must've heard me! Of course he would think I was a man! A girl could *never* fly through the sky on a magic sleigh! A girl can't even be a carter on the ground!'

'*Santa must be the name of the mysterious man,*' Blanche read aloud, '*because it fits with the letters signed S CLAUS.*'

Carol sat in awkward silence. 'Poker Carol is going to feel terrible,' she finally muttered.

'Poker Carol?' Blanche asked. 'What's he got to do with it?'

'Oh, you know,' Carol said casually, as if it weren't a big deal. 'Carol with the fire poker did some enthusiastic skewering when sending the letters and skewered all the Ms off. To be fair to him, it was very unlikely to matter at the time.'

Blanche flopped back on the bed as Carol nervously thumbed through a few more newspapers.

'Oh look, there's a new angle in this one,' she said, trying to cheer Blanche up. 'The man who heard "Santa" also told how the sleigh got out of control briefly and one of the reindeer lost its nametag. He found a broken section of it outside his door. The reindeer is called—'

Carol stopped and scrunched the paper into a ball.

Blanche sat up. 'What? Carol, give it to me!'

Carol shook her head and shoved the paper in her mouth. 'Mits mot mimmormant.'

'It *is* important,' Blanche said. 'Spit it out.'

Carol did as she was told.

Blanche furiously smoothed it out and scanned the article.

'RUDOLPH?!' They've made *Rudy* a boy too!'

'Again,' Carol said, 'I don't think it'll catch on.'

Santa arrived and instantly felt he had done something wrong.

'The Captor has ruined everything!' Carol seethed, relishing a chance to be angry with him again.

'It's not his fault,' Blanche said, patting the bed for Santa to sit down.

Santa read the newspaper stories, his face pained. 'Oh no, I've ruined it.'

'It's *not* your fault,' Blanche said, 'and I won't have you feeling bad about it. All across the world children are marvelling at their presents, and that is exactly what we wanted. I just wish someone could have looked up into the sky and seen a girl driving the sleigh.'

'I could tell the papers they've got it wrong,' Santa suggested. 'I could sail back to London and explain.'

Blanche shook her head. 'You hate sailing! And you love it here. Anyway, you can't speak to the papers – they wouldn't believe you. Or they would and then they

would hound you forever, until they discovered Carolburg and the elves and ruined everything we've made.'

She lay back with a sigh. But she thought of Rinki and the mince-pie picnic and all that they had dreamed up so far. She didn't feel defeated, she felt more determined than ever to change the stories.

'Tomorrow,' she said, 'we'd better get to work.'

Carol held up a newspaper. A drawing took up the whole front page. A drawing of Santa.

'Well, one positive is they got your teeth right,' Carol said, moving the paper next to Blanche's face.

Blanche shot her a look.

'I'm an eighty-year-old man with a beard, Carol!'

ONE (ALMOST) CHRISTMAS LATER ...

Chapter 39

Truth Disappearing

M r Krampus had been very busy in the year since he saw 'Santa'. As the newspaper responsible for revealing the identity of S. Claus, everyone turned to him for more news – but he didn't have any, so he made things up.

SANTA CLAUS SAYS BADLY BEHAVED
CHILDREN WILL GET COAL INSTEAD OF
PRESENTS!

Blanche was furious when Rinki sent her that one.

'I would NEVER say that!' she cried.

'Ugh,' Blanche groaned, tossing the paper aside. 'That has Mr Krampus written all over it.'

The carter boys had also been busy. They knew the real identity of the mysterious Claus, and they knew Mr Krampus was wrong. So – armed with the newspaper clipping in which Mr Krampus had once promised a reward for revealing the mysterious figure's true identity – they made their way to Stratton Street.

Little did they know as they walked past number 6 that they were walking past the very building – the very roof! – where Blanche and Rinki had dreamed the whole plan up in the first place.

They knocked boldly on Mr Krampus's door. It was a skull door knocker, but that didn't faze them.

'YES?' Mr Krampus bellowed as he threw the door open.

Whipper held the newspaper clipping up to the man's face. Or as close as he could get, given he was half

his size. He just about managed to stretch past Mr Krampus's elbow. 'We're here about the reward.'

Mr Krampus waved his hand dismissively. 'That's an article from last year. Claus's identity has already been revealed – by *me*. Didn't you hear?'

'We did,' Cole said. 'But you got it wrong.'

Mr Krampus's face grew darker.

'You got her name wrong and everything,' Sprout said. 'Claus is the carter girl from the docks. Goes by the name Flimp.'

'Utter nonsense!' Mr Krampus cried.

Whipper shook his head. 'No, Mr Krampus. Saw it with my own eyes I did. Well, *eye*. I had the other closed. I was peekin'.'

'The girl with the mangy old horse and the battered cart?' Mr Krampus spat. 'Have you *seen* the sleigh Santa rides in?'

Whipper nodded. 'She must've upgraded it.'

'The carter is a *girl*,' Mr Krampus sneered.

'We know *that*,' Sprout said. 'It was you who told us!'

'My point,' Mr Krampus said, losing the little patience he possessed, 'is that a girl COULD NOT POSSIBLY BE

THE MAN FLYING THROUGH THE SKY!'

'She is a really good carter,' Cole said, getting a kick from the others for saying so. 'What?' he protested. 'She *is*.'

Mr Krampus went to close the door.

'What if we proved it?'

Mr Krampus paused. 'How?'

'When Christmas comes, we'll bring her to you,' Whipper said. 'Plus the sleigh, the horse and the truth.'

'And ... we'll have our reward?' Sprout said hopefully.

Mr Krampus considered the offer for a moment. He very much doubted they were right, but if they were, that posed a problem – he'd be made a fool of. If they were right, he'd have to bury the truth, and that carter girl with it, once and for all. 'Very well,' he said. 'You have a deal. Now get off my street, you're making it look hideous!'

Chapter 40

Christmas, Again

It was Christmas Eve and Blanche was soaring over London.

The skies were clear and icy-cold and the streets were decorated with yesterday's snow.

Blanche had got faster, and slicker. She leaned over the edge of the sleigh as they flew over Green Park and spotted Rinki, as arranged, staring up at her favourite statue. She pulled on the left rein and looped back round to land.

Her best friend was wearing her purple cape with the sequin angel wings, which billowed in the wind. Her hair was shorter and she'd grown taller since their last meeting.

They both stared up at the statue.

'I can't believe they think I'm a man,' Blanche said with a sigh.

Rinki patted Blanche's face warmer. 'The beard probably doesn't help!'

Blanche pulled it off. 'I could be a girl with a beard!'

'I have an idea,' Rinki said, holding out her hand for it.

Blanche watched as she made her way to the statue and began climbing it.

'What are you doing?' she cried.

At the top, Rinki swung around Boudicca and stood in front of the two sculpted figures sitting in the back of the chariot. She looped the beard around one of them.

'I always wondered who this other figure would become,' Rinki said. 'We knew it was you up front driving and I was in the back. Now we know the one next to me is Santa, your other best friend. So if the world thinks Santa has a beard, then we should put the beard on him!'

Blanche laughed as she held out a hand to help Rinki down.

The snow began to fall again as she looked up wistfully at the statue. Blanche, Rinki and Santa – and they were there all along.

'I want to show you something,' Rinki said, pulling Blanche through the park. 'It'll only take a moment.'

They ran through the empty streets, stopping outside the department store where they'd bought presents two years before.

A sign that read *SANTA'S GROTTO* hung in the window.

'When I came to do my Christmas shopping last week, the queue stretched to the butcher's and beyond,' Rinki said. 'I went inside to get a better look. It was a cave filled with puffs of fake snow and a man in a red suit, though not nearly as fabulous as the one you wear.'

Blanche sighed. 'As much as Carol protests, I think the Santa thing might be catching on.'

'Another year or two and then everyone will know the truth,' Rinki said optimistically. 'They will know that Santa is real and wonderful, but so is the girl who delivers the gifts.'

They returned to the sleigh. Blanche was going to

Rinki's house for their mince-pie picnic, but there was one stop she had to make first – her final one in London. She promised Rinki she wouldn't be long.

At the docks, she touched down on the roof of the old stone tack hut and made her way down the chimney. The three boys seemed fast asleep, curled up in the corner like they had been the year before.

Blanche opened the sack of presents, but before she could reach inside, she heard a crunch behind her. She whipped round but it was too late. Something hard hit her head and the floor leaped up to meet her.

Everything was spinning. She could feel hands on her and shouts of 'GET THE HORSE DOWN FROM THE ROOF!'

Her legs felt weak and no matter how much she ground her palms into the cold floor, she couldn't lift herself up.

She heard a thump and then the sound of thirty-six hooves clattering outside, the crunch of a sleigh on snow and bells on antlers. They echoed in her head, getting more ghostly and slow as the room spun faster and faster, and then disappeared into darkness.

Chapter 41
The Men in Suits

When Blanche woke, she was tied to a chair with reins. Whipper, Cole and Sprout loomed over her.

'Rudy,' Blanche tried to say, but it came out as a croak. Her mouth was dry and her lip throbbed and tasted of blood.

'Where are you?' came a voice. It wasn't one of the boys, but it was someone just as familiar.

'Carol?' Blanche groaned quietly. She wanted to shout, but she didn't have the energy.

Whipper held up a limp sack in front of her and jiggled it.

'Blanche?' came Carol's voice again. 'BLANCHE? EVERYTHING SOUNDS VERY MUFFLED! We're seeing if we can do anything, and when I have an update, I'll—'

'Carol,' Blanche managed a little louder, realising the bauble from Rudy's nose was in the sack. 'I'm—'

But before she could heave the words out, Whipper placed the sack on the ground and stomped on it. The bauble crunched painfully under his heel and Blanche listened in horror to Carol's voice stretch and shrink until it was gone.

She was alone, and no one knew she was in trouble.

'Wait till Mr Krampus sees this! We're going to be rich!'

Blanche stared at the boys. She wanted to leap up and scream but her head pounded, and if she was going to lurch her body into action it wasn't going to be for a scream.

'Please,' she begged. 'Not Mr Krampus.'

'You know,' Whipper said, 'this is the second time you've fooled everyone into thinking you're not a girl.'

Blanche gritted her teeth. 'That wasn't my intention this time.'

'Well, then you won't mind telling Mr Krampus,' Sprout said. 'You can correct his mistake for him!'

Blanche could feel the panic rising. She wriggled furiously, shouting for Rinki and Santa and Carol.

'Someone doesn't like Mr Krampus,' Whipper teased.

'Please,' Blanche said. 'We all know he's never going to admit he was wrong, even if he does know the truth. He'll never embarrass himself like that. Who knows what he'll do to me!'

'We just want the reward,' Cole said with a shrug.

'Consider it repayment, Flimp,' Sprout said, 'for stealing all our jobs!'

The boys laughed, and that was when Blanche saw two very familiar figures emerge from the shadows.

'The strange men in suits,' she whispered in disbelief.

'The what?' Whipper said.

After that, everything was a blur. The men in suits made a grab for the boys while Blanche tipped the chair on its side and wriggled towards the door. She fought with the reins that tied her, pulling and stretching until

the heat against her wrists was so fierce she thought they might burst into flames. There was a snapping sound and Blanche ripped herself free, just as Whipper fell to the ground beside her. She leaped to her feet and backed into the wall.

'Out cold,' one of the strange men hissed, nodding at the boys.

'Who are you?' she said to the suited men, moving around the edge of the hut, inching closer to the door. 'I don't have the box!'

The men didn't answer. They came so close that Blanche could see the dark dead space beneath their hats.

She screamed and grabbed the first object that came to hand – a saddle. She lifted it high in the air and swung it with all her might, striking both of them with one blow. There was a thump as they crumpled to the floor. She closed her eyes, wincing at what she'd just done, but when she opened them again, the men were gone.

In their place were two small creatures Blanche knew very well.

'Carols!' Blanche cried, scooping up the little

274

fairies. 'Where did the men in suits go? What are you doing here?'

The Carols looked confused. 'How does she know our names?' one whispered to the other.

'I liked that suit,' said the other grumpily. 'I wanted to be a strange man in a suit for longer.'

'Wait a second!' Blanche cried, placing the Carols back on the floor. 'The strange men in suits were you all along?'

'We're on a secret rescue mission to bring Carol home. We thought we heard her voice. We know she's in here and we will not give up until you give her to us!' He stretched an arm up to waggle a finger in Blanche's face. He barely reached her ankle. 'Where's the box?'

Blanche picked up the sack and tipped out the glowing red shards.

'You heard her voice through this. I hate to be the one to tell you, but the Carol you're trying to rescue is back in the North Pole,' Blanche said. 'And she's been back there for a long time.'

The Carols looked at each other.

Blanche could tell they were unsure whether to

believe her or not and realised she had to prove herself to them somehow.

'I know that you turn into elves in very cold temperatures,' she said.

'Everyone knows *that*,' one of the Carols said. 'Einfrieren Little Fairy.'

Blanche thought again. 'I know about Carolburg and Snowcus Pocus. And I know about Eggnog.'

The Carols whispered to each other.

'Are you sure that wasn't a guess?' one of them asked.

'He likes to roll down the mountain without his ornaments on and it causes avalanches.'

'I think she's telling the truth. Eggnog is *niche*,' the fairy said.

Blanche smiled. 'None of the other Carols thought to tell you that Carol was home and safe?'

'Well, we've been undercover – self-appointed. Uncontactable! Incognito!'

'We told no one where we were going. We've been gone for ages – had to do Snowcus Pocus in a London park and everything,' the other Carol said, almost proudly.

'We've been completely stealth! Under a rock! Nothing but shadows! Off the grid!' the other went on, until his friend nudged him to stop.

'We need to pick up our things from our spy post on Stratton Street and then head back to Carolburg,' the Carol said. 'Thank you for the very useful information.' And with that they flew out into the night.

'Wait!' Blanche cried.

Rudy stuck her head round the door and neighed – it sounded unlike any neigh Rudy had made before, all wobbled and worried.

'Oh, Rudy!' Blanche cried. 'Thank goodness they didn't hurt you.'

The reindeer stood in the snow outside, looking furious on Blanche's behalf. The boys were still out cold, in the corner where they had been pretending to sleep when she first arrived.

'Where's the sleigh?' she asked, stepping outside. She froze and let out a whimper. The sleigh was ruined – the boys had hacked away at it and ripped out the seating, and it felt like they had ripped Blanche's heart out too. Half of one side, once a glorious shiny red, was now nothing but snapped wood and splinters.

Rudy looked to Blanche for guidance.

'We're going to see Rinki,' Blanche said. 'She always makes everything better, and anyway, I won't miss our mince-pie picnic.'

Chapter 42

Great Darkness

Rudy and the reindeer helped pull what was left of the sleigh through the empty streets of London towards Rinki's house. Exhausted, Blanche threw her arm around Rudy's neck and the horse helped keep her steady as they walked through the park and up Stratton Street. They were quite a sight, and children waiting up late in their windows for a glimpse of Santa were quick to spot them. They ran outside in their pyjamas and slippers until the street was filled with pyjama-clad helpers.

'It's Santa, but ... it's a girl!' they said excitedly as they lined up behind the sleigh and pushed.

'Oh look!' shouted a man from his window. 'Santa's sent his wife this year and she's crashed the sleigh!'

'I didn't crash it!' Blanche shouted back. 'And I'm not Santa's wife!'

'SHE'S A TERRIBLE DRIVER!'

Rinki threw the door open and came charging into the street in her nightgown.

'Blanche?' she cried. 'What happened?'

She ran around the sleigh to look inside.

'It's ruined,' she concluded. 'Who did this to you? To the sleigh? To *Christmas*?'

There was a fury and power in her voice that Blanche had never heard before, and it felt warm and comforting in the icy wind.

'The carter boys,' Blanche said. 'They tried to capture me and bring me to Mr Krampus.'

Rinki groaned and began piecing bits of the sleigh back together with a determined look on her face. 'Well, don't worry about Mr Krampus – I gave him the rest of the Brussels Sprout Brew from last year, so he's all tucked up in bed.'

Blanche kicked the sleigh. She'd forgotten about the Brussels Sprout Brew. Even if the carter boys had dragged her to his horrible house, the beast would have been out for the count.

The children in their pyjamas helped with the sleigh too, and they were making great progress until the distant sound of charging hooves and carts skidding through snow made them stop.

'Oh no,' Blanche whispered. It was a sound that had chased her for years, and now it looked like it had caught her.

'The carters are coming,' Rinki said urgently. 'Quickly, children, inside the house, where it's safe!'

Blanche could hear Rinki, but her words floated somewhere just out of reach. She could feel that she was on the edge of another moment that would change everything. Only this time it didn't feel good.

I see great darkness.

Great darkness.

Great darkness echoed over and over in Blanche's mind until she felt frozen to the ground.

'BLANCHE!' she could hear Rinki shouting. The sound of clattering hooves and whips filled Blanche's head until she couldn't hear Rinki any more.

She felt a tug on her cape and looked down to see a little boy in teddy bear pyjamas smiling up at her. 'It will be OK,' he whispered.

It brought Blanche to her senses.

She quickly lifted the little boy and carried him to the safety of the house.

'I think that's all of them,' Rinki said, checking the street for stragglers.

'YOU?' came an astonished shout from behind them, making them jump. 'It's *you*?'

Blanche turned to see Mr Krampus, and she was sure the many terrifying eyes on his cane narrowed at the sight of her. Mr Krampus was certainly livid at the sight himself – he looked from her to the reindeer and sleigh and back again in utter disbelief.

'But … the Brussels Sprout Brew! You should be asleep!' Rinki said. Then her eyes widened as if something terrible had occurred to her. 'Keeps for up to a year! The brew was out of date!'

The carter boys rounded the corner.

Mr Krampus walked fast towards them, his face red with rage and his cane raised high in the air, like a pitch-fork ready to skewer them.

'You? Two girls? You're behind all this?' It was more unbelievable to him than flying reindeer.

'Surprise!' Rinki shouted furiously.

Mr Krampus stepped closer to Rinki, forcing her to move back, her heels balancing precariously on the edge of the pavement.

The carter boys were almost upon them. Mr Krampus raised his cane.

Blanche froze in horror, realising what was about to happen but unable to stop it.

Rinki's eyes grew wide and her face seemed to crack like ice. She looked to her friend for help. Blanche skidded through the snow. A gleeful grin spread across Mr Krampus's face as he tightened his grip on his cane and then pushed it hard into Rinki's chest.

'No!' Blanche cried, but it was too late.

Rinki fell into the road and the carts crashed down on top of her.

Cook chased the carter boys down the street at record speed, armed with a half-cooked turkey. She eventually caught them in the park, next to Rinki's favourite statue.

Blanche lay in the snow with Rinki, two broken snow angels together, and wished she could make everything better.

'The filthy, rotten carters did it!' Mr Krampus was saying to Captain Garland. 'Hideous, the crimes they commit!'

Blanche could hear Mr Krampus's words echoing around her, but she didn't feel like she was there. She squeezed her friend's hand tightly, and then she remembered something.

'CAROLS!' she roared, leaping to her feet.

Mr Krampus sniggered. 'Carols?'

'I really don't think this is the time for singing, Blanche,' Captain Garland said quietly.

'CAROLS!' she shouted again, more urgently.

'You called?' came a little voice from across the street.

Mr Krampus turned as white as the snow. 'Tiny demons,' he whimpered.

'Einfrieren Little Fairies, actually,' one corrected him.

'Oh look!' cried the other, pressing his face to Rinki's. 'Who did this horrible thing?'

'Mr Krampus did it,' Blanche said, and with a *pop!* and a flash of candy-cane coloured light, Mr Krampus was tied up with tinsel.

'We,' the fairy said pointedly, 'will deal with *you* later.'

They huddled over Rinki.

'Can you do something?' Blanche said. 'With your magic?'

The fairy held Rinki's hand and his hair flashed a candy-cane colour, but she didn't wake up.

The other Carol cracked his knuckles. A flash of candy-cane light lit up the sky, but Rinki still didn't wake up.

'We're going to need the best Carol we've got,' one of the Carols said. 'We need … Carol.'

'The one from the box,' the other clarified.

'But she's in Carolburg … the North Pole,' Blanche said.

Teddy came slipping through the snow. 'Our carriage is trapped by snow! The servants are digging it out!' He fell to his knees and held on tightly to Rinki's hand. 'We'll

get you help, just hang on.' He was in such shock he hadn't even noticed the little fairies standing in the snow.

'I know I can save her,' Blanche told Teddy and the captain. 'But not here. Can I take her with me?'

Captain Garland looked up to the sky. 'I have always believed in magic,' he said. 'And I believe in you, Blanche. You're the best chance we've got.'

'We trust you, Blanche,' Teddy whispered.

He reluctantly let go of Rinki's hand and helped Blanche carry her to the broken sleigh.

With a quick flash of candy-cane light, the sleigh was transformed to its former glory.

The world was deathly silent as Blanche gathered up the reins. And, without so much as a TALLY-HO, she took off.

Only the children huddled at the study window noticed that Mr Krampus had slipped out of the tinsel restraints and disappeared.

As Blanche flew through the sky, news of who really rides the sleigh spread among the children of London

and beyond in quiet whispers. They knew that it was Blanche Claus who delivered their presents. She and her best friend dreamed it up together.

The girls of Christmas.

Chapter 43

Two Things

There was just enough magic left to fly them home, though they had to walk the last mile.

When Blanche arrived, she was exhausted, with icicles hanging from her eyebrows and a look so sad it made Santa burst out crying.

It was Christmas Day, and Snowcus Pocus came quickly enough for Carol to get to work on Rinki.

Blanche watched hopelessly as candy-cane coloured light shot through the sky again and again, until all the technicolor lights of Carolburg exploded and the city fell into darkness.

'Great darkness,' astrologer Carol whispered to

Blanche with a knowing nod.

Carol stepped away from Rinki. 'I've done all I can. Now we wait.'

Blanche sat in the snow by her best friend's side. She lay on a bed of ice, surrounded by snowmen and a thousand elves, who hoped with all their might that Rinki would wake up.

'What if she never wakes up?' Blanche sobbed. 'Rinki befriended me, no questions asked. Everything we created we created together, and without her it doesn't make sense. She *was* Christmas to me!'

Carol gestured for the other elves to leave. Santa got up too.

'You can stay, Santa,' Carol said, making him burst out crying all over again. It was the nicest thing Carol had ever said to him.

'We wanted to change the world for the better,' Blanche said, her voice shaking. 'So why does it feel like I've only made things worse?'

'Blanche, we just need to wait now,' Carol said.

'I have two things to show you,' Santa said. 'I think they might help a little.'

Blanche reluctantly followed his candlelight, her boots dragging through the snow. She turned and saw Carol was trying to keep up, but using all her magic on Rinki had taken its toll and the poor little elf looked limp and grey. Blanche scooped her up and cuddled her close.

Elves popped their heads out of their windows and watched as Santa led Blanche through the maze of snow-topped houses to Christmas Lodge.

Eggnog was standing there.

'I CAN AND I DID, BLANCHE!' Eggnog said. 'I CAN AND I DID!'

The fir tree was standing tall and proud, with not a single speck of destruction around him.

'He's been practising while you've been away,' Santa said.

'He hasn't broken *anything*,' Carol added. 'You taught him that.'

Blanche raced towards the tree and gave him a big hug, snuggling into his warm fir. His decorations jingled as he lifted Blanche up and then placed her gently back in the snow.

'And he hugs, but not forever now,' Carol said.

Eggnog tapped the very tip of his head, where someone had placed a gold star. 'LOOK, BLANCHE, CAROL GAVE ME A STAR FOR GOOD HUGS!'

'Thank you,' Blanche mouthed at Santa.

'Oh, we're not finished!' Santa said. 'We have one more thing!' He nodded at Eggnog and the tree stepped aside.

Behind him stood a huge ice sculpture – an exact replica of Rinki's favourite statue in London.

She reminds me of you.

Santa looked expectantly at Blanche.

'Rinki sent a tinsel letter and asked me to make it for you,' he tentatively explained. 'For your Christmas present. She said you'd know what it was.'

A moment passed before Blanche finally cried, 'THIS DOESN'T HELP!' Tears began streaming down her face.

Carol tutted and stared angrily at Santa. 'This is *classic* Captor.'

Santa looked panicked. 'I'm sorry, I just thought—'

'IT'S THE MOST HEARTBREAKING THING I'VE EVER SEEN!' Blanche wailed.

'Oh, really?' came a familiar voice from behind her. 'I was absolutely sure you'd love it.'

Blanche whipped round.

Rinki was standing in the snow.

'Merry Christmas, Blanche,' she whispered with a smile.

Blanche had a wonderful Christmas showing Rinki the sights of Carolburg.

'And now we've got the two rogue elves back,' Carol said, 'they can stop using their magic to make themselves into sinister suited men and instead fly Rinki here and back once a year!'

Blanche was surprised. 'Rinki can visit? Every year?'

Carol nodded. 'We'll send the rogue elves in the sleigh to collect her.'

They were back in front of the ice statue, admiring Santa's skills.

'The carving is phenomenal,' Rinki said, making him blush.

'It was nothing,' he said. 'Just four thousand hours of

solid work, and I almost lost a thumb. But who needs a thumb!'

'In London, we decided that one is you, Santa,' Blanche said, pointing at the second figure in the back of the chariot. 'We even put the face warmer on it and laughed about how everyone thinks I'm you and that you're an old bearded man.'

An elf stepped forward with another face warmer and Santa gave Blanche a leg up. She looped it over the ice figure's head and climbed back down to Rinki. Her heart felt mended in so many different ways all at once.

'I feel very honoured to be up there,' Santa said, 'with the girls who conquered Christmas.'

At that moment, the letters for next Christmas burst through the doors, whipping around them like a flurry of snow.

'Well,' Blanche said. 'We'd better get to work.'

Chapter 44

Through the Years

Every Christmas Eve until she was old and grey, Blanche Claus would fly across snowy skies and climb down every chimney. And every year, Santa would hand her a flask of hot chocolate and the snack-filled stocking with the B he had sewn on the front, just for her.

She got faster and faster as the world grew, and every year she would visit the old stone tack hut, delivering presents to new carter boys, until the hut didn't exist any more.

When Rinki grew up she became the head of the London Costume Society – and she changed the way

women dressed forever. She made trousers popular, and she travelled the world for inspiration – sometimes hitching a ride with Blanche on Christmas Eve. She made sure her life was always full of magic, and many, many mince pies.

Mr Krampus disappeared and never returned to Stratton Street, leaving his house and his fortune behind in an attempt to evade justice. He knew the true identity of Claus, but Christmas after Christmas passed and he never revealed it. The success of two formidable girls was not a tale he wanted to tell. And so he untangled himself from their story and decided he would forget them.

But the problem with having a determined nemesis with a flying sleigh is that eventually you will be found. Luckily there was a sheet of floating punishment ice the elves had no use for any more.

Cook took over Mr Krampus's empty house and turned it into a year-round Christmas restaurant. She called it The Christmas Lunch Club, after her painting from Teddy, and Rinki decorated every inch of it with her tinsel letters.

Cook took in the carter boys, because she knew she could set them right. She taught them everything she knew and grew very fond of them. Whipper was good at whipping cream, Cole was hot on roasting things, and Sprout? Well, he mostly liked folding napkins.

The elves spent every Christmas Eve reading Eggnog bedtime stories to send him to sleep. Then Carol would wrap his new decorations and line them up neatly at the end of his bed, ready to open in the morning. He had his elf family, and they had him.

Captain Garland and Teddy never took the Christmas tree down at 6 Stratton Street, and the strange box with the iron stars sat in the study for as many years as they did. But no Einfrieren Little Fairy was ever locked in it again.

Many years later, Blanche's old bridge was demolished, and little Christmas Lodge along with it. A new bridge was built in its place – and it was built by women.

Then one snowy and special Christmas Eve, when the sky was clear and decorated with every star, an elderly Rinki walked with the red bauble dangling from her finger.

It was time.

She stopped and gave it to a young child waiting for her parents on the corner where Christmas trees are sold.

'Never underestimate the gifts you are given,' she whispered mysteriously. 'Merry Christmas.'

Up above them, a sleigh pulled by reindeer – and Rudy – shot through the sky. Old Blanche looked down at her friend and waved.

They had a mince-pie picnic to get to.

Epilogue

Dear You,

I AM INVENTOR CAROL AND I HAVE A MISSION
FOR YOU! When I invented tinsel paper, it was
harmless and wonderful and a great way for Blanche
and Rinki to communicate and still keep our world
a secret. But over the years, tinsel has snowballed in
the human world. They changed it and now they
like to make it out of a strange sparkly plastic. The
problem is this plastic hurts the creatures of the world –
it takes hundreds of years to biodegrade, and can you
imagine how many pieces of tinsel there are in the world

if everyone uses it on their Christmas tree?

Your mission is to help me invent some tinsel that is good for the environment. We need our planet – without it, there will be no Christmas.

Thank you for listening.

Also, I invented video games, so you all owe me one.

And never forget – if you find a red bauble, be sure to look and see, because there might just be a snowy world and a dancing fir tree …

Until Christmas,
Carol (the inventor one)

The Truth about Eggnog!

An Extra Jolly Bonus Story

Now, Carol doesn't lie as such, but she has occasionally been known to bend the truth, which means there's a little more to the Eggnog story than she'd have you believe. But since it's Christmas, I'm sure she wouldn't mind me telling the *whole* story …

There was a blizzard the day Carol created Eggnog. A blizzard so thick that all the elves looked like miniature misshapen snowmen toddling around town, and Carolburg itself was nothing more than a white lump on the landscape.

It also happened to be Carol's birthday.

She maintains that she created Eggnog because she wanted a friend, and that *is* partly true. Who would say no to one more friend? But even Carol isn't so silly as to pick the HUGEST tree in the forest and think, *I'll bring that one to life, that's a foolproof idea.*

Her reason for bringing a tree to life – giving it a mouth and a personality and the ability to uproot itself and go wherever it pleases – can be summed up in six words:

POLAR TAVERN CANDY-CANE-EATING COMPETITION.

It's a legendary competition – candy-cane-eating at its most extreme.

Every year on her birthday, Carol marches to the Polar Tavern and tries to win the coveted Polar Tavern Candy-Cane-Eating Competition Candy Cane of Champion Chomping. But every year she loses, because she's very small. And polar bears are not.

After carefully studying the rules, Carol realised the only rule about magic was that an elf must not use magic on themselves during the contest. (This amendment to the rules was the result of one naughty elf, who shall remain nameless, magically adding four extra mouths to his face to increase his chances of winning). Crucially though, there was no rule against magicking up a substantial-sized friend and having them stand in for you in the competition. The rules stated that you could nominate a CHAMPION.

So that morning, Carol set off to find a polar-bear-sized tree. She found the perfect one, right on the edge of the forest, standing small in comparison to the much larger trees behind it.

Although the elf rules forbade magic, Carol imagined that once she arrived home with the coveted Polar Tavern Candy-Cane-Eating Competition Candy Cane of Champion Chomping, all would be forgiven. Every elf in Carolburg dreamed of putting that candy-cane trophy in the town square. She'd be a hero! And because it was her birthday, she wouldn't get into trouble, because no one is allowed to get you in trouble on your birthday even if you do break the elf rules, go rogue and win a candy-cane-eating competition with a large talking tree.

Unfortunately, when doing a little magic to make the tree come to life, the blizzard turned its blizzarding up a notch. Carol was propelled left, and then left again, and finally forward, until she was smooshed into the largest tree in the forest.

It began to glow and, well, you know the rest. It came to life.

'Well,' Carol said, trying to look on the bright side, 'at least I'll definitely win the competition now …'

'I ONLY WANT TO DO THE COMPETITION IF I CAN WEAR SOMETHING FUN,' the tree insisted after Carol had explained what she needed him to do. So Carol rushed back into town and fetched him some decorations.

Happy with his new look, he scooped Carol up and they jingled all the way to the Polar Tavern – a series of igloos filled with a warm glow and many polar bears glugging from large mugs. It's loud and growly, but mostly a friendly place – until the candy-cane-eating competition starts.

Carol skipped in and grabbed a candy cane from the counter, throwing it down on the floor.

'Oh, it's you,' a polar bear said. 'We end up eating so many candy canes on this day every year because of

you. But very well, we will choose a champion to chomp against you.'

A very large polar bear thudded a paw down in front of Carol, making her spring up and hit the ceiling.

'And I will choose *my* champion!' she said gleefully as she plummeted back down to the ground.

The polar bears laughed. 'No one here will be your champion,' one growled. 'We polar bears stick together.'

There was a rumble outside and the roof began to shake.

Carol grinned so widely that the corners of her mouth went all the way past her ears, making her hat pop off.

'What is going o—' the polar bear began, just as the roof of the igloo was smashed open.

'HELLO ... JUMBO FURRY ELVES WITH CLAWS!' came a bellowing voice, making the polar bears' fur blow back. 'I'M HERE TO EAT CANDY CANES!'

The polar bears gulped.

And so the candy-cane-eating competition began: polar bear versus magic tree. The weirdest festive-themed eating competition the world had never seen.

A huge platter of candy canes was placed in front of

each contestant, and on the growl of three they began to EAT!

At first it looked like the polar bear might win. The tree started by gently licking the candy canes and in no time at all the polar bear was on to his second platter. Then his third.

'MMM,' the tree said, putting two of them in his mouth like fangs. 'I HAVE LONG TEETH!'

Carol jumped up and down at his side. 'Chomp them! Chomp them!' she cried desperately.

The tree raised a bushy eyebrow. 'OH,' he said, finally realising what he needed to do.

Then he gobbled the lot.

And the rest of the platters – before they could even be served to him.

The polar bear slumped on the table and raised a paw in defeat.

'You … you did it!' Carol cried, tears of joy streaming down her face. She leaped up and hugged the tree. 'You're the best friend an elf could have!'

'I still think it's sort of cheating,' a polar bear mumbled.

'THE CHAMPIONS!' another cried. 'Carol and …
what's the tree's name?'

Carol and the tree looked blankly at one another.

'MY NAME? I DON'T KNOW!' the tree fretted.

Carol grabbed the Polar Tavern menu and scanned
the drinks.

'Eggnog.' She smiled. 'His name is Eggnog!'

And that is how Eggnog came to be both a giant
enchanted Christmas tree *and* Carol's Polar Tavern
Candy-Cane-Eating Competition Champion Chomper
of Candy Canes.

It had been the best birthday of Carol's life, and
together she and Eggnog walked home through the
thick blizzard, with Carol perched on his head like a
magical menace of a star.

'We're back, Eggnog,' Carol said, looking down at
Carolburg and all the snow-covered elves peering up at
her in horror. 'We're home.'

And even from way up high on Eggnog's head,
she could hear the familiar screeches of,
'CAAAARRRROOOOOLLLLL! WHAT HAVE YOU
DONE?!'

WITCH WARS

Read the whole ritzy, glitzy, witchy series!

AVAILABLE NOW!

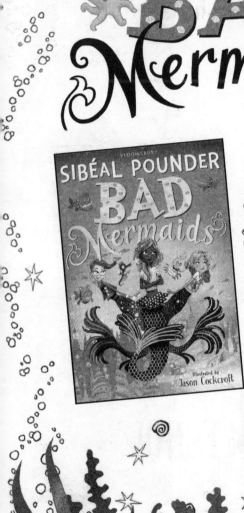

Read the whole fabulously fishy series!

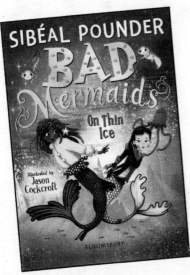

AVAILABLE NOW!